A first kiss almost two decades in the making.

It was worth every minute of the delay. Delicious and tempting her to want it to never end. Kissing Patrick awakened sensations that had been missing from her life for a while. She'd barely noticed men since everything in her life fell apart, but Rhiann was certainly noticing Patrick now.

She'd been so focused on Levi and just surviving that she'd barely managed to function. The only thing further from her mind than dating had been falling in love again. But the moment his lips touched hers, she wanted things.

…Like promises and forevers.

Patrick eased back. When their lips parted, they stared at each other, trying to process all the emotion and change that came with a kiss of that magnitude. His stunned expression told her he was as shocked by the kiss as she was. He probably hadn't expected everything that kiss had held, either.

Dear Reader,

After a tragedy, sometimes it can be hard to look forward. So what happens when you open your eyes and see your future tangled with all the painful memories of the past?

Patrick has sworn off relationships in every way, wanting to protect his heart from the pain of further loss. Rhiann is a single mom, determined to get her son the care he needs, even if that means facing her once best friend, now sworn enemy. Despite his determination to push people away, he has a hard time resisting her pleas to help her son. Even as they grow closer taking care of her son, their shared past stands between them.

Thank you for picking up *Heart Surgeon's Second Chance*. This story made me laugh, it made me cry, and I hope that you will enjoy reading Patrick and Rhiann's story as much as I enjoyed writing it. I love hearing from my readers, so if you'd like to get in touch you can find me @AllieKAuthor on Facebook, Twitter or Instagram.

Happy reading!

Allie

HEART SURGEON'S SECOND CHANCE

ALLIE KINCHELOE

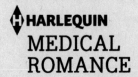

HARLEQUIN
MEDICAL
ROMANCE

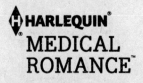

HARLEQUIN®
MEDICAL
ROMANCE™

Recycling programs
for this product may
not exist in your area.

ISBN-13: 978-1-335-14934-3

Heart Surgeon's Second Chance

Copyright © 2020 by Allie Kincheloe

This edition published by arrangement with Harlequin Books S.A.

For questions and comments about the quality of this book,
please contact us at CustomerService@Harlequin.com.

Harlequin Enterprises ULC
22 Adelaide St. West, 40th Floor
Toronto, Ontario M5H 4E3, Canada
www.Harlequin.com

Printed in U.S.A.

Allie Kincheloe has been writing stories as long as she can remember, and somehow, they always become romances. Always a Kentucky girl at heart, she now lives in Tennessee with her husband, children and a growing menagerie of pets. Visit her on Twitter: @AllieKAuthor.

Heart Surgeon's Second Chance
is Allie Kincheloe's debut title for Harlequin.

Visit the Author Profile page at Harlequin.com.

This book is dedicated to all those who have helped me along the way, my family and those who have become like family—you know who you are.

And to Victoria Britton—without your belief in this story, this book wouldn't exist.

CHAPTER ONE

Rhiann

DREAD POOLED LOW in Rhiann's stomach as the door to the exam room opened with a slow and ominous creak. Broad shoulders in a white coat filled the space and her eyes roamed the doctor's familiar form, taking in the subtle changes time had wrought.

Three years ago he hadn't had those deep lines etched into his face. His dark hair had a little more silver at the temple than she remembered, but he was as lean and handsome as ever.

Dr. Patrick Scott stepped into the room, his eyes looking down at the screen of the silver laptop in his hand. His movements carried the spicy aroma of his cologne into the small room, the pleasing notes covering the harsh antiseptic and teasing a part of her that had gone dormant since her divorce.

But on top of the overtly masculine scent he

brought with him a wave of sadness that hinted at tragedy.

"Hello, Mrs…. Masters…um…"

His deep gravelly voice trailed off and his sky-blue eyes jerked up to meet hers when he recognized her name. The slight fake smile he'd had on his lips when he'd opened the door faded fast. Judging from the ice that frosted over his gaze, the animosity he held for her hadn't eased since she'd last seen him.

The exam room door shut behind him with an audible click and the laptop clattered slightly as he set it roughly on the counter.

"What are you doing here?"

The uncharacteristic coldness in his tone sent a shiver coursing down her spine. Patrick's voice had always held such emotion, its rich timbre broadcasting his feelings with the simplest words. In all the years she'd known him Rhiann had never heard this distant tone.

Rhiann hugged the baby in her arms close to her chest, tears filling her eyes as she fought to keep her emotions from overwhelming her. She'd hoped the time since they'd last seen each other might have given Patrick clarity and smoothed the raw edges of his anger, but clearly not enough time had passed. Now she could only hope that he would be professional enough to put their personal grievances aside and focus on her child's best interests.

She needed to keep a clear head today, so she stuffed her feelings away as best she could. She had known coming here was a risk, but there was no other way or she'd have explored it already.

"I need your help. Well, he needs your help. This is my son Levi. He has a heart defect, and the cardiologist at St. Thomas' wants to do surgery to fix it. But if anyone is cutting my baby open I want it to be the best surgeon I can find." She paused to swallow down an oversized lump in her throat. "And that's you."

"You expect me to save someone you love. How ironic."

A single dark eyebrow raised as he stared down at her, his expression unreadable and as cold as marble. His eyes searched hers—for what, she didn't know.

Just as she was sure he was about to tell her to leave, to scream at her like he had the last time she'd seen him, his gaze flicked down to the baby in her arms and the ice in his eyes melted the tiniest bit.

"Please, Dr. Scott."

The formality felt stiff and awkward as it rolled off her tongue without the teasing tone she'd used each time she'd called him by his title in the past. Years ago they had been the closest of friends, sharing every secret with each other. They had even flirted with the idea of a relationship on an occasion or two.

But it no longer seemed appropriate to call him by his given name. Not when their friendship had crumbled on the back of accusations and misplaced blame. Their personal connection was more of a hindrance than a help in her quest to get her son the care he needed, so she kept things formal, hoping to appeal to his professional side.

His eyes snapped up to meet hers and that hint of softening was gone. "You ask too much."

The once happy-go-lucky Patrick had earned a reputation over the last couple years for taciturnity. His white-hot talent was tempered by his ice-cold bedside manner, but he was the best pediatric cardiac surgeon in the southeast, and that fact made people overlook his brusque manner.

He'd changed three years ago—just as she had.

Rhiann remembered the caring man he'd used to be, though, and she hoped there was enough of that man left deep inside for him to agree to help. Her son's life depended on it.

"Maybe I shouldn't have come here, but I had to try. I had to give my sweet baby every chance possible. Because he's just a baby."

She reached for any way to connect with the man standing before her, sensing that rejection sat poised on his lips.

"Look at him. He's an innocent child who needs your assistance. Can you live with yourself if you don't at least try to help him?"

"I'll have my partner—"

"I didn't come here for your partner. And even though I know he's an excellent surgeon, I refuse to let you pass Levi off to Clay. Because I came here for the best surgeon I know. Not for second-best."

He muttered a curse, so low it was barely perceptible, and pinched the bridge of his nose. "You know if he needs surgery we'll be seeing each other a lot over the coming weeks and months? Do you know what seeing you that often is going to do to me?"

Clearly not a single thing had changed between them. He still hated her. But that fact changed nothing about her mission today.

Emotions threatened to clog her throat and Rhiann coughed a bit to clear it. She swiped at a hot tear that had leaked from her eye and run down her cheek. With a hard inhalation she tried to lock those feelings away, because she needed to keep a cool head. She had to convince Patrick to help Levi.

"Whatever you think I did or didn't do, that

was in the past and between us. It has nothing to do with my son. I've run that day through my head no less than a thousand times, but there's nothing I could have done that would have changed anything. I can't change the past, but you can change Levi's future. You can *give* him a future."

His brows furrowed, Patrick pressed his lips together tightly, but her words must have touched something in the man she'd once known because he was pulling his stethoscope from around his neck.

"Let me take a look at him, run a few tests, and we'll go from there. His records from his previous doctors haven't been transferred yet, and I'd like to review those as well."

"That's all I ask."

Rhiann's heart thudded in her chest as Patrick sat on a rolling stool and pushed it over to listen to Levi's heart. His hand brushed hers, warm despite his cold manner, as he moved the stethoscope gently over her son's back. He sat close, his knee bumping into her thigh when he shifted to listen to Levi's chest.

She inhaled sharply at the touch and he looked up at the sound, their gazes meeting over Levi's head. The spark that fired up in his eyes brought back a time when distance between them hadn't existed and their lives had been far easier, and she wished they could return to the easy-going camaraderie of those days.

The exam room suddenly shrank in size as new strain filled the space and fire warred with the ice in Patrick's eyes.

The silence amped up the tension until finally he snapped back to the present enough to speak. "What tests has he had done? And how recently?"

"Most recently he's had chest X-rays and an EKG. Two weeks ago."

Rhiann swallowed hard. Her own medical training made this harder, because as a paramedic she knew enough to know that Levi's heart condition was really bad.

"They told me Levi had a heart murmur when he was born—but a lot of babies have murmurs, you know? So, I was watching it, but it only kept getting worse. Then he started turning blue, and I knew it was more than just a murmur. I pushed and pushed until we saw a specialist. Six months ago he had a shunt put in that was supposed to help. But, as you can see from his coloring, it's not enough. I'm not even sure the shunt has helped at all."

"I'm not sure it has either."

Patrick rolled the stool over to his computer and Rhiann breathed deeply for the first time since she'd made the appointment to see him.

The keys clicked and clacked beneath Patrick's nimble fingers as he made some notes on Levi's chart.

He spoke without looking at her. "You might want to have Pete with you for the tests, for emotional support. How's he handling all this, anyway?"

"I have no idea. Pete sent me divorce papers shortly after Levi was born. I haven't seen or heard from him since before Levi had his shunt put in. Last I heard he had moved back home to California and was living near his parents. Despite loving all the music here, you know he always hated Nashville. Not close enough to the water for him. And once he gave up on the idea of a music career—well, I'm afraid it's just me and Levi now."

Patrick spun on the stool and stared at her for a minute. "I didn't know," he finally acknowledged.

"Well, now you do."

Patrick had never liked Pete, so it would surely make him happy to hear that he'd been right when he'd warned her it would never last. The teensiest bit of joy flashed in his eyes and his lips curled up momentarily before he brought his emotions back under the icy veneer.

Her spine stiffened as she waited for the *I told you so* from her former friend.

"What happened?"

She sighed and let an abbreviated version of the story slip past her lips—a story she'd told more than once. "I had a hard time getting pregnant. We needed help from a donor. Pete never really connected with the thought of a baby that wasn't his biological child, and… Well, when the news came in that Levi wasn't absolutely perfect, that he had a heart problem, Pete just couldn't escape fast enough."

Levi was her family now. The only person in the world she had to love and to love her in return. She didn't need a man like Pete. She didn't need anyone at all except Levi. And for Levi she'd cross as many rivers and boundaries as she had to in order to get him the help he needed.

Right now Levi needed the surgeon sitting in front of her, and she was definitely crossing over the boundary lines he'd thrown up between them. Not just crossing them, but stomping on them and maybe setting them on fire for good measure.

Patrick snorted. "If only someone had told you that loser wasn't worth your time…"

Despite expecting the rebuke, the frigidness in his tone shocked her. Rhiann blinked away more tears. The man sitting before her bore little resemblance to the friend she'd once known.

That man would never have spoken to her with such vehemence.

She hugged Levi closer, knowing she couldn't leave here without Patrick agreeing to help her son, and determined to take whatever Patrick felt he had to dish out in order to make that happen.

Very little in her life had come easily, and if there was one thing she knew it was how to stay strong and fight for what mattered. Levi was worth every fight she'd faced already, and he'd remain worth any fights there were to come.

The baby squeaked in protest as she unconsciously tightened her grip on him as she stiffened up her resolve. She eased her hold and rested her cheek on the top of Levi's head, murmuring an apology.

She'd surprised Patrick, based on how his body stiffened beneath her hand when she reached over and put her hand on his white-cotton-clad forearm. His arm was warm beneath her fingers, which was surprising, since she'd almost expected his arm to feel like solid ice to match his demeanor.

"You can fix him, right?"

Patrick

Emotions rolled over Patrick. Waves of anger swirled around spikes of sympathy, and even a hint of something he didn't want to put a name to. He shut his feelings down and didn't allow himself the luxury of emotions.

No feelings meant no pain. And if anyone had ever perfected the art of depriving themselves of all emotion it was Patrick.

He pushed the stool back away from the teary-eyed blonde and her tiny son before the sweet scent of vanilla and apricots that wafted from her overwhelmed his sensibilities and made him do something stupid.

Like pull her into his arms and whisper reassurances about her son's future that he wasn't sure he could fulfill. Or kiss her to see if she still used the strawberry lip gloss he'd been so desperate to taste once upon a time.

He cleared his throat and pulled up the cold professionalism that had served him well these last few years. No matter how good Rhiann smelled, no matter how many sparks shot up from his arm at her simple touch, he would not allow himself to think of her that way—not her, not after what she'd done.

"I don't want to make any promises until I see exactly what we're looking at. But I don't like what I'm hearing. You have to know that Levi's in poor condition."

From what he'd heard of the little guy's heart, surgery was almost a guarantee. But promises were wasted words when he was talking about a heart the size of a plum. And, with their past, if Rhiann had sought him out, surely she already knew things were bad.

"I can't lose him," she whispered, her lips feathering across the baby's forehead. The shadows in her eyes darkened as she processed his words. "He's all I have. Please, help him."

A mother's love visibly permeated her every move. It had brought her here today, despite knowing she'd have to face him again. That courage ripped open something deep in Patrick's chest, and he knew it would take more than a hastily slapped-on bandage to patch the gaping hole Rhiann's reappearance in his life had rent.

He stood abruptly, the stool rolling back into the wall with a rattling thud that echoed in the quiet stillness of the exam room. Fighting back the emotion that Rhiann kissing her child had triggered, he snapped out a quick response. "Levi needs an echo and a heart catherization. Once we get the results of those, we can go from there. I'll have my nurse schedule the tests."

Leaving the door to slam shut behind his rushed exit, Patrick strode down the hall to the nurses' station. He shoved the laptop across the counter. "Schedule these tests for Exam Three and get them out of here now."

He turned toward his office, heedless of the

stares coming from his staff, but he didn't miss the muttered conversation behind him.

"I wonder what the mom in three said that turned the temp down on the Ice Castle? Geez…"

"Right? I didn't know he *could* get any colder."

He ignored their words and walked away.

Thankfully, Levi had been his last patient of the day. Shutting the door, Patrick leaned back against the smooth wood and closed his eyes, trying to shove all the pain back into the depths of his mind. He tugged at the tie around his neck, loosening the silk that threatened his air supply.

Nothing could have prepared him for Rhiann's return to his life.

Nothing.

Inhaling deeply, he focused on the abstract painting behind his desk. His late wife had painted the simple lines, with bold and contrasting colors, to help ground him when he found himself overwhelmed by the emotions and heartbreak that came with being a pediatric heart surgeon. Mallory had been deeply aware of his need to keep his environment outside the operating room calm. She'd known him better than he'd known himself at times.

He followed the lines across the canvas with his eyes, from light to dark, then back to light, while he took several slow, deep breaths.

He had to pull it together.

His nerve endings were twitching at the memories assaulting his consciousness, overpowering his present with painful reminders of the past.

Of all the people to walk into his practice today, it had had to be Rhiann—the one person he'd never wanted to see again. He'd wanted to rage at her and have her removed from his sight. He'd wanted to pull her into his arms and find out just what her perfectly pink lips tasted like.

There was just something about her... Something that had always fascinated him almost as much as it had angered him. Rhiann had been his first crush, his unattainable first love, but they'd never been on the same page when it came to a relationship. Then he'd met Mallory, and Rhiann's role as his best friend had been locked in.

At least until she'd betrayed his trust...

And now *she* had to be the first woman to catch his interest in three years.

The dark shadows under her eyes told him she wasn't sleeping, and he didn't have to wonder why. The way her clothes hung off a frame much thinner than he remembered had brought back protective instincts he would rather not have had reawakened.

Just for that he wanted to hate Rhiann.

Hate her for making him *feel*.

He'd tried not to notice how Levi's illness was

affecting her. They weren't friends anymore and it shouldn't matter to him at all that she'd lost the dead weight from her life by divorcing that idiot Pete.

But it did matter.

Too much.

He'd almost told her to get out.

Almost.

But then he'd looked down at the little boy in her arms and found himself unable to banish her from his life once more. When he'd opened his mouth to tell her to go he'd heard himself say instead that they'd run some tests. Why? Because the blue tint to her tiny son's skin reminded him of who he was and why Rhiann had come back into his life. And, regardless of how Rhiann had betrayed him, he couldn't take all that resentment out on an innocent baby. Even if he wanted to hurt her like she'd hurt him, he couldn't bring himself to say no to Levi.

Instead of being a robust and active toddler, the frail eighteen-month-old Levi was the size of a nine-month-old. His little heart wasn't pumping right and his every breath seemed a struggle.

He hadn't got out of Rhiann's lap to run around the exam room. He hadn't crinkled the paper on the table with delighted giggles. He hadn't torn pages from the books and magazines.

No, he'd only sat in Rhiann's arms and barely reacted to the exam.

Levi was a very sick little boy who urgently needed Patrick's help. And he'd help Levi. But not because he was Rhiann's son. He'd help Levi because it was the right thing to do, both as a physician and as a human being. He'd help Levi and then Rhiann could get out of his life once more, like he wanted.

Seeing Levi snuggle into Rhiann's embrace had triggered a heated assault on his emotions. The wall of ice surrounding Patrick's heart had thickened again, though, when he'd read Levi's birthdate on the chart. It was exactly two years later than his own daughter's due date.

But his sweet little Everly had never drawn a breath.

Everly would never snuggle into his embrace.

And the woman who had just begged him to save her son's life had been the one who'd cost him everything.

With a single angry gesture he swept everything from his desk into the floor. Files and stationery fluttered down without much sound, but the metal organizer tray clattered as it hit the floor and bounced.

A tentative knock preceded a soft, "Are you okay in there, Dr. Scott?"

"Leave me alone," he snarled in response.

The "Jerk…" his nurse muttered was only just audible.

He sank down onto the floor and leaned against the door. Taking some deep breaths, he stared at the platinum band on his left hand. His whispered words were too soft for anyone outside to hear.

"I miss you so much, Mallory. I don't know how to go on without you."

CHAPTER TWO

Rhiann

WITH THE WAY Patrick had run out of that exam room like someone had set his lab coat on fire, Rhiann wasn't entirely certain that she'd gotten through to him. Before he'd rushed out she'd been certain she'd glimpsed a crack in his frozen façade, but now, as the days passed without a word, worry crept in and set up shop.

If Patrick wouldn't help Levi she had to come up with a backup plan. She was all he had, and she refused to let him down.

On the fifth business day after Levi's appointment her patience ran out. When she stopped for lunch, she steeled her nerves to call his office and check in. Holding a finger against the twitch at the corner of her eye, Rhiann learned they had already scheduled Levi's echocardiogram.

And, of course, it was smack-dab in the middle of one of her shifts at work.

Before she could ask to reschedule, her partner shouted over that they had a call and she had to hang up quickly. She shoved the last of her sandwich into her mouth and ran over to Charlie and their rig.

In the three years she'd been a paramedic with County Hospital, Charlie had been her partner. He'd been with County for seventeen years and, beyond having become one of her closest friends, the older man had quickly become her mentor and the nearest thing she had to a father figure.

She had never known her father—that deadbeat having left before she was born. Her mom had told everyone in town she had been widowed while pregnant—not that anyone had believed that. They'd lived in a small but immaculately clean trailer for the entirety of her childhood.

An only child of an only child, Rhiann had never had any other family. That had changed when she'd met Patrick.

Unlike her, Patrick had grown up in an affluent two-parent family. While his mom had never worked, his father had been an award-winning podiatrist. They'd been able to afford sports and extracurricular activities, private tutors, and anything else their son had needed. But, despite her being from a vastly different social class, his parents had always been kind to her, the poor girl from the outskirts of town.

Now her family circle had dwindled down to more of a triangle. She had Levi, and she had Charlie. And that had to be enough. Because she couldn't risk the damage to her heart if another man let her down.

Dispatch sent them out to a minor car accident, and after that to a nasty burn. Rhiann used the time between calls to tell Charlie about the upcoming tests and surgery.

"How much is all that gonna cost?" Charlie asked. "Sounds like a whole bucket of expensive to me."

He winced when Rhiann listed off the estimates that the calculator on the insurance website had given her. She'd flinched too when she'd seen the numbers.

"I'll figure it out somehow," Rhiann said, gnawing on her lower lip.

The tests and the surgery were going to break her already fragile financial equilibrium, but what choice did she have? Levi needed them, so she'd make it happen. She'd pick up as much overtime as she could, and she'd set up a payment plan with the hospital—like she'd done for his shunt surgery.

Next month, that would finally be paid off. She'd been looking forward to having a larger food budget again, but that was clearly not meant to be. Yet she knew she'd make it.

Charlie looked over from the driver's seat, a kindhearted look on his age-lined face. "You always do, but it sure would be easier if you had some help."

Rhiann sighed, ignoring Charlie's last comment. Pete had no interest in helping support Levi. He had zero interest in being part of Levi's life. She'd only learned after her separation how little Charlie and the rest of her coworkers had thought of her now ex-husband. The station house had even had a running bet on just how long her marriage would last.

Charlie had won two hundred and thirty bucks for his guess. When she'd found out about it she'd made him take her out to dinner with some of the money before she'd forgiven him for betting on her marital status.

"So, this old doctor friend of yours is going to fix our boy up, right?"

"If anyone can, it's Patrick."

She might not have confidence in a lot of things, but she was confident in Patrick's abilities. Seeing him again, even if it had been hard, had felt good. They'd gotten that first awkward meeting over with now, and maybe someday they could work toward being friends again. He'd looked good, even with the uncharacteristic coldness of his personality, and that new touch of gray in his hair added a distinguished vibe she really liked too.

"What's that blush about? You hot under your uniform collar for a dude in a lab coat?"

"I am nothing of the sort!"

Rhiann slugged him on his shoulder and laughed. She and Charlie had an easy-going camaraderie that allowed for a lot of teasing. In some ways Charlie had filled a little of the void Patrick's absence had left in her life. But not entirely. No one could replace Patrick, after all.

He laughed. "That pink in your cheeks tells me enough—now tell me about your doc."

"He's not *mine*."

"So you've said." Charlie snorted. "But that pretty shade of embarrassment darkening up your cheeks tells me that you want him to be."

She looked away, staring out the window as they drove back to the station where both the paramedics and the firefighters for the county were based. She wanted to argue, but she didn't like to lie to Charlie. So she kept her mouth shut for the remainder of the drive.

They had only just pulled in to the station when Dispatch sent them straight back out.

"Couple of teens shooting things out over at the county line..." The voice on the radio crackled out the info and the address followed.

"I hate these calls," said Charlie, and turned the rig around with a sigh.

He flipped on the lights and sirens as they hurried toward the given address. They kept quiet as they headed to the scene, taking the time to mentally prepare themselves for what they might find. Kids and guns—it was never a good combination.

The address was a gas station just off I-24, and the lot was full as Charlie eased in, trying to find their patient through the crowd of people.

"There," Rhiann said, pointing to an older sedan with a shattered window near the air pump at the back corner of the lot.

A boy around thirteen, maybe fourteen, lay on the oily pavement next to the rusted car. Blood pooled around his right leg, and the bright red was a dismal sign, even as a young woman pressed what looked to be a jacket to the wound.

Rhiann hopped out of the rig and grabbed her kit.

"I think it hit a vein or an artery or something," the woman said.

Only a few years older than the boy lying on the pavement, the young woman was about three shades too pale. From experience, Rhiann knew that the shock of this was going to hit the woman hard once the adrenaline rush was over.

"Do you know his name?" Rhiann asked as she gloved up.

"Naw, I never seen him before today. I was just getting air in my tire when he came running up and some guy shot at him. I saw how he was bleeding—there was just so much blood—I took a first aid class and they said to put pressure on wounds, but I didn't have anything but my hoodie, and—" She finally ran out of air and stopped to take a shuddering breath.

Rhiann had some gauze pads ready. "Okay, you did really good. On the count of three, I want you to take your hoodie away and I'm going to take over, okay? One, two, *three*."

On three, the woman pulled the ruined hoodie away, and Rhiann got her first view of the kid's thigh. A large gaping hole exposed not only injured muscle, but a damaged femoral artery, and blood squirted out with every erratic pump of his heart.

"Charlie!" Rhiann shouted. "Nicked his femoral!"

She reached in and pinched the artery closed with her fingers. With her free hand, she fumbled through her bag.

"I can't find any clamps that will hold in the position of the damage. We need to get him to a surgeon and fast—before he bleeds out."

Charlie brought the gurney over and they

carefully loaded the teen. Once they got him into the rig, Charlie got an IV started and hopped into the driver's seat.

"Dispatch, this is Rig Three. That kid you called us out to is in bad shape. Requesting permission to transport to Metro or Vanderbilt, because County's not going to be able to handle this. They need to have a surgeon meet us, because my partner's holding this kid's femoral artery in her hand and he's already lost a lot of blood."

Rhiann swallowed hard, feeling the nerves filling her when Dispatch gave Charlie the go-ahead to transport their patient to Metro. Every time a call took them to Metro she worried that Patrick would be in the Emergency Room when they rolled in. But only once had she caught a glimpse of him from a distance, and he hadn't seen her.

Shaking her head, she returned her full focus to the patient in front of her. "Charlie, you better be standing on that gas pedal, or this kid doesn't have much of a chance."

Patrick

"Dr. Scott, we have a three-year-old with a possible murmur. Would you mind taking a look?"

Dr. Dixon's grating nasally voice had called

from behind him. Patrick stopped and spun toward the ER attending, who had stopped his escape from the hospital after rounds.

"Who's on call from Cardio?"

"Belcher. We've paged him three times, though, and he hasn't responded. I just don't want to discharge this kid if there's something serious and I——"

Holding a hand up, Patrick cut the younger doctor off mid-ramble. "I got it. You're trying to cover your own butt since Belcher isn't here to do it for you."

The attending's ears reddened at the accusation that Patrick had thrown at him, but he didn't deny it.

"Is that a no?" Dixon asked.

"I'll take a look. Where's the patient?"

The attending handed him a file, relief obvious on his face. "He's in Curtain Two."

"I'll find you when I'm done."

He strode to Curtain Two, where a cursory check told him the boy was fine. He heard no sign of a murmur at all. He'd just shoved the file back into the attending's hands when a trauma page came from overhead.

"Ready, Trauma Bay One. Ready, Trauma Bay One. Incoming. ETA: two minutes."

Nurses and doctors came from other rooms

and started readying themselves for the incoming ambulance.

"What do we have?" asked, Dr. Abbott, head of trauma.

"Teen with a gunshot wound, possible femoral involvement," one of the nurses said, gloving up and putting a gown over her scrubs. "Probably going to be a messy one."

When he saw the rig that pulled in didn't have an MMH logo on the side Patrick's curiosity was piqued and he stayed to watch the trauma. But when the doors opened and Rhiann sat straddling the patient, her hand inside the gaping wound on the teenager's thigh, watching was no longer an option.

Shoving his hands into gloves and quickly donning a gown, he moved to support her as they lowered the gurney from the ambulance.

"I've got a young male, approximately thirteen years of age, name unknown. Large-caliber gunshot wound to the upper thigh. The bullet nicked the femoral artery and he lost probably a fourth of his volume at the scene. I couldn't get a clamp on the bleeder, due to the damage, so I'm currently providing manual pressure. He's been in and out of consciousness—mostly out."

Rhiann rattled off stats as they pushed her and the teen through the doors into the trauma bay.

Her face was pinched and the tension in her arm worried him. "Is your hand cramping?"

"Getting there." She looked up, their eyes meeting. "I'm tightening up, for sure."

He grabbed some lap pads and moved closer, trying to get a view of what they had to work with in the kid's thigh. "His thigh is trashed."

"I couldn't get a clamp on. The artery is almost shredded under my hand."

Patrick had an idea. "What if I clamp above and—?"

"Below? And that will let me get out of the way." She finished his sentence, nodding her agreement with his idea. "And hopefully that will hold until—"

"Until they can get him upstairs and into an OR." He returned the favor and finished her sentence.

A nurse held a clamp out to him and he took it. He nearly had to lay his head on Rhiann's shoulder in order to get close enough to get visibility and a good angle on the artery. He clamped it just above her hand.

"Clamp one is in."

He held his hand out for another clamp. Once the metal instrument was in his palm, he moved closer.

"I'm going beneath your hand now, Rhiann. I'm have to get in real close to be able to see."

He bent down, his head wedged beneath her arm as he tried to see in the shadows.

"Can I get some more light?"

Someone angled one of the moveable overhead lamps.

"Thanks," he murmured.

His face was close enough to Rhiann's side that he could feel her breathing, her inhaled breaths bringing her uniform shirt into contact with his cheek. With the back of his wrist he nudged her arm, and she responded by moving it up slightly. It was just enough that he could get the clamp onto the artery, below where her fingers were pinched.

"Okay, I think you can let go now."

Rhiann eased her hand away from the open wound, and when the artery didn't spray blood the nurses in the room began to clap.

"That was amazing. It's like the two of you were sharing a brain," Dixon commented.

Patrick helped Rhiann off the gurney. As soon as she was clear the teenager was rolled out of the room, rushed straight for the OR, where surgeons would fix what Patrick and Rhiann had only temporarily patched.

Rhiann was flexing and relaxing her stiff hand. She turned away, taking her gloves off and dropping them into the bin.

He followed suit before spontaneously grabbing her hand. He massaged it to help loosen the stiffness. "How long were you holding that kid's life in your hands?"

"About five minutes?" She shrugged, sighing when his fingers touched a particularly sensitive spot in her sore hand. "I'm not sure of any details right now except that your fingers are magic."

He ignored her words and focused on getting the last bit of tension out of her hand. "You saved that boy's life," he told her.

And she had. Her quick thinking in grabbing that artery with her hands had been the only thing standing between that kid and meeting his maker. Because of her this boy would leave the hospital—and not in a body bag.

"You helped." She grinned up at him, her eyes bright and full of accomplishment. "I thought my hand was about to fall off before you got that artery clamped."

Abbott slapped Patrick on the back. "Man, it was good to see the two of you working together again. As morbid as this sounds, I miss the days of you two being in my ER regularly, and seeing you work like a precisely calibrated machine to save a kid's life."

As Abbott's words sank in the fun of the save faded and Patrick remembered exactly why they didn't work together anymore. The recollection of why everything had changed flooded his mind. His chest tightened at the onslaught of painful memories.

He dropped Rhiann's hand as if she'd burned him and stepped away He glared at Abbott, who flinched under the scrutiny. "Those days are long past and you'd do well to forget them."

He left the trauma bay, hands fisted at his side, anger with himself tightening his muscles. He'd let himself get caught up in the adrenaline rush that a trauma could bring. Let himself enjoy the camaraderie and familiarity of working side by side with Rhiann again and let himself trust her every move.

But he couldn't trust her.

How could he have forgotten that?

CHAPTER THREE

Patrick

PATRICK AND CLAY were following a nurse's instructions to the staff lounge on the main floor at County. He hadn't spent enough time at this hospital to know his way around, despite having had surgical privileges there for years.

"Man, I hope there's some coffee in this place." Clay fidgeted with the strap of his bag and yawned loudly. "I'm getting too old for these early mornings."

Patrick raised a brow at his partner. "You aren't old yet. And it's not early—in fact, it's almost noon."

Clay grinned at him. "I didn't get home until after midnight, and when I was in bed I wasn't asleep for some time. I need coffee, but I'm not turning into a pumpkin just yet."

Rolling his eyes, Patrick pushed open the door marked *Employees Only.* "You go from Cinderella to the Wicked Witch when you haven't got enough sleep."

"My preferred comparison is Dr. Jekyll and Mr. Hyde, thank you very much."

Patrick walked into the small room and set his bag on a table along one side. "Oh, good—there's coffee."

A feminine voice from the corner stopped him just as his hand closed on the handle. "I wouldn't do that if I were you."

He released the pot and spun around, because he knew that voice.

"Rhiann!" Clay had already stepped forward and was greeting Rhiann like an old friend. "I haven't seen you in so long. How are you?"

"Hi, Clay." She accepted Clay's outstretched hands and held them for a moment before looking in Patrick's direction. "I'm doing okay."

"How's Levi?" Patrick asked.

"We had the EKG this morning. They said they'd send his results over to you as soon as they're ready."

He nodded. "Okay…good."

"Who's Levi?" Clay asked, looking between Patrick and Rhiann.

"My son. He has something going on with his heart."

Her eyes met Patrick's and the certainty he saw there was humbling.

"But if anyone can fix him it's Patrick."

Parents came to him because of his reputation. They brought their babies to him because his record spoke for him. He got results. He saved more children than he lost. They trusted his medical skills even though they'd never met him.

This was different.

Rhiann trusted *him*. Not the world-renowned doctor with awards and plaques hanging on the walls of his state-of-the-art office. She didn't know or care about the number of articles he'd published in prestigious medical journals or his presentations at top conferences.

No. She trusted Patrick the man.

Despite barely speaking to him for three years, she still trusted him. And that realization brought a lump to his throat that he didn't want to acknowledge.

"What are you doing here?" Clay asked, pulling Patrick away from his introspection as Rhiann broke eye contact.

"We're on the clock. Waiting on a transfer. The floor doesn't have her ready for us yet, so we thought we'd grab a coffee while we waited."

She waved a hand down at herself. The dark uniform suited her. Her hair was up in a professional-looking twist that left her neck bare… perfect for kissing.

He inhaled sharply. Where had *that* thought come from?

The older man in the corner cleared his throat. "You might have to grab a gurney and push me down to the ED after this." He held up a plastic cup filled with dark liquid. "That coffee's done put hair on my chest. I'm not sure how it hasn't eaten through this cup yet, but I'm pretty darn sure it's made its way through my esophagus."

The man wore a uniform that matched Rhiann's. He reclined back, legs outstretched, and faked a moan. "It's killed me, I tell you."

Rhiann rolled her eyes and snorted. "And that's my partner, Charlie. If there's drama to be found, Charlie's in it up to his ankles."

"Hey!" Charlie protested.

"Fine—up to his knees." She smiled indulgently at Charlie, her affection for the older man shining brightly in her eyes.

"Better," Charlie agreed, nodding his head in her direction before throwing the rest of the coffee back like it was a shot. "Gah! Who needs whiskey when you have County coffee? It burns all the same going down."

"Don't worry, old man, I have your antacids out in the rig." Rhiann laughed at her partner's antics. Then she turned to Patrick with a smile on her face. "See why I warned you off that stuff?"

"Is there anywhere close where we can get some decent coffee?" Patrick jerked his head toward Clay. "That guy might implode if I don't get some caffeine in him soon."

Rhiann shook her head sadly. "Not in this hospital."

"Close by?"

She pursed her lips in disgust. "Not for miles. They like it strong enough that the spoon bends around here. Charlie still tries to drink it, but I've learned my lesson. I think it's probably too strong for your tastes too. But you might try the nurses' station up by the trauma ICU. They've been known to make a fresh pot for Charlie when he flirts a little. They might even wash the pot for you two."

Clay winked at her. "Thanks, doll. I always did like you. I'm gonna go see if I can sweet-talk a nurse into a coffee." He slapped Patrick on the shoulder. "I've got my cell—call me when they're ready for us."

"What are you guys doing all the way out here at County, anyway?" Rhiann asked. "Metro Memorial is your stomping ground."

Patrick shrugged. He leaned a hip against the counter. "Usually. But they don't have a pediatric cardiologist who has done a heart transplant on staff here at the moment, and I still have privileges, so when they needed a procurement team they gave me a call."

Her eyes teared up. "Someone's losing their kid today?"

"Several more are having their kids saved today."

He always tried to focus on the positives, because that was the only way he could get through the day when he had to do a transplant surgery. He focused on how many people each donor had saved, because otherwise he had to remember the pain that came with being a donor's family. Knowing that Mallory's last act on earth had been to give life to others had been the only thing that had got him through when he'd lost her.

"How many?" She grabbed a tissue and dabbed at her eyes.

He'd always loved her eyes, the bright green of new spring grass, and the tears in them now made the color even more vivid.

"I'm not sure." He thought back to all that he'd been told in the phone call. "I don't remember. I know the heart is going to a seven-year-old in Ohio. And the lungs to a nine-year-old in Pennsylvania."

"Small comfort, I suppose."

She smiled at him, but the sadness radiating from her eyes penetrated deep into his soul. She looked as if the world had just collapsed on her and she couldn't hold it up any longer.

Rhiann had always been so strong, but there was an air of fragility to her now.

He pushed away from the counter and laid a hand on her shoulder, trying unsuccessfully to ignore the frailness in her frame. "You okay?"

She nodded.

Charlie's radio crackled behind them, alerting them that their patient was now ready for transport.

"We need to go, Rhiann."

Patrick wanted to say more, but he didn't know where to begin or how to condense it down into a moment or two. His mouth opened and closed with no sound while Rhiann gazed up at him. Those big green eyes had been rendering him stupid for years, and it seemed they hadn't lost their power over him.

"I've got to go."

She gave him a quick hug and was gone again before he could return the gesture. Her arms around him had stunned him, and he couldn't process the feel of her softness pressed against him before she'd moved away and the entire moment was gone.

Clay came back in as Rhiann and Charlie rushed out.

"I come bearing gifts." He held out a cup of

steaming coffee. "Rhiann was right—the nurses up there are incredibly friendly. I walked away with coffee for us both and three phone numbers."

Patrick took the coffee and sank down into a chair with a sigh.

"Wanna talk about that hug I just saw?" asked Clay.

He shook his head. There was no way he could talk about what he himself was struggling to understand. Having Rhiann's arms around him had him so mixed up it was like he had been thrown in a blender. How could he want to hug someone he had sworn to hate?

"No? How do you feel about Rhiann reappearing in your life?"

Patrick lowered his eyes to the coffee in his hand. "I don't want to talk about that either," he growled out.

"You haven't seen her in a long time. You have to be feeling *something* about her showing up after so long. She was your best friend for half your life." He paused. "Still don't wanna talk? Okay, I'll talk. You listen."

Clay moved a chair until he was sitting directly in front of Patrick.

"Your best friend there still wants to be a part of your life. You need to pull your head out of your nether regions long enough so that you can see that."

He took a sip of his coffee and stared at Patrick until the urge to squirm was almost more than he could bear. Clay had a gift for making anyone feel like a child with a simple raised brow.

"I can't trust her. She let—"

"I know what you *think* she did, and I still maintain that you're wrong—because Rhiann is a walking heart. She cares too much about everyone she meets. I know she would have done everything possible, even if you are too stubborn to see that." Clay plowed over Patrick's objections like an unsubtle bulldozer. "What if Rhiann has come back into your life for a reason?"

"What are you suggesting?"

"I'm not *suggesting* anything. I'm *saying* outright that you need to forgive her. And you need to forgive yourself for not being there when Mallory and Everly died. You couldn't have saved them, and you need to accept that Rhiann couldn't either."

"I didn't ask for your advice." Patrick stood up, intending to put some space between himself and his annoying partner.

Clay rose to his feet and blocked the only exit. "And yet I'm still offering it—and it's because you need to hear it. These last three years you've been grieving, and I gave you space to do that.

But all this negativity is eating you alive, man. You have to stop just existing and move forward with your life. Do you think Mallory would be happy about how you've been living? About you being alone and shutting everyone out?"

"Clay—"

"Mallory would be heartbroken at the thought of you freezing out your best friend over her. She knew how much Rhiann meant to you." Clay got one more stab in. "I'm surprised that you've forgotten."

"Shut up, Clay."

But Clay continued, "I think that woman holds the key to your future happiness in the palm of her tiny little hand, and I think you are too smart to lose her twice."

Patrick's phone buzzed with the notification that their patient was ready for them. He glared at his partner and changed the subject. "We need to go scrub."

Clay tossed his cup into the trash and gave Patrick a somber look. "Once again, saved by the bell. One day you won't be so lucky. You'll have to face your past and learn to forgive."

Rhiann

Rhiann could tell by the number of glances that her partner kept sneaking in her direction that he had something to say. The older man was not known for subtlety, but he'd wait until they had a modicum of privacy before he unleashed his opinion on her.

Thankfully they had a patient who was not only awake, but chatty, so that should buy her a little time while she tried to figure out just what had happened in that break room with Patrick.

They were transporting an elderly woman back to her assisted living facility after a short hospital stay.

"Tell me something good," the lady said, reaching out to pat Rhiann's arm with her age-spotted hand. "I've got to go back to the home with all those old biddies who have nothing better to do than compare whose health is worse."

"I don't know much that's good right now. I'm not the one to ask." Rhiann laughed a wry, humorless laugh. "I can switch spots with Charlie and you can do a little flirting, though?"

"You'll do no such thing. I remember Charlie when he was hiding behind his mama's skirts. I can no sooner flirt with that child than I can run a marathon." She clucked her disapproval. "What kind of woman do you take me for? I'm no cradle-robber."

Rhiann met Charlie's gaze in the mirror, smiling at the hint of red she saw tingeing his cheeks. "Oh, really? Maybe you're the one who needs to tell *me* something good, then. You have any dirt on my partner that I might use to my advantage?"

"You could tell her about that pair of doctors you were getting friendly with while we waited on her to get ready," Charlie said loudly. "I'm sure she would rather hear about two handsome single doctors who got a little handsy with you in the break room than tell a story about me when I was a snot-nosed brat."

"Oh, yes? Are you being courted by two doctors?" Their patient's furrowed face lit with excitement. "Do tell me. I love a good romance."

Rhiann sighed, not wanting to disappoint the old woman. "There is no romance."

"You only say that because you didn't see the look in that man's eyes when he thought you weren't watching." Charlie snorted. "If I could show you what I saw…"

A wrinkly hand waved, urging Rhiann to spill her story. "If you don't tell me I'll get Charlie to—and, while I know his version will be quite entertaining, it will only contain a hint of the truth."

Rhiann pinched the bridge of her nose. "Fine. But there is no romance."

"Let me be the judge."

"The abbreviated version is that the two doctors are old friends of mine—Patrick and Clay.

I met Patrick in high school, where we became best friends from day one. He went off to med school while I stayed here locally, and when he came back it was with a wife and Clay. We were all friends for some time, and then something tragic happened. Patrick's wife and daughter..." She trailed off, unable to finish that part of the story. She wrapped up her tale in a no-nonsense, definitive tone. "Now we aren't friends anymore. See, I told you—no romance."

"Hmm..." the woman said. "That's quite a story you've told in only a few words there."

"You notice she only really told you about one of them. Right?" Charlie said.

Rhiann closed her eyes and sighed. "Charlie..." she warned.

"She only told you about one because she barely saw the other one. I was only teasing about her having the two of them after her. Even if poor Clay was interested he doesn't stand a chance—not standing next to Patrick."

"It sounds like there are a lot of strong emotions on both sides," the elderly lady said wisely.

"Hate is definitely a strong emotion," Rhiann agreed.

"Except hate is *not* what that man's feeling for you."

"Shut up, Charlie."

Charlie laughed from the front of the rig. "She

got a little emotional and he nearly launched himself across the room to comfort her. Couldn't help himself—he just had to touch her. That's not how a man reacts to someone he can't stand. Even if he hasn't admitted to himself that he's got feelings for her, let me tell you, he's got them."

"My mama, God rest her soul, always used to say you couldn't have hate without love," said their patient. She shifted on the gurney. "I believe that's true. Maybe the boy had to hate you so he could see how much he loves you now."

Rhiann shook her head. "You're as bad as Charlie, aren't you?" She ignored the hope that was trying to blossom in her heart like a stray flower in the crack of a city sidewalk. "I'm going to tell you what I tell him—and that's that I don't have time for romance. There's no room in my life for a bunch of hopes and dreams I have no control over. The only man I have room for in my life is my son, and I don't need anyone else."

"Pshaw! You're too young to be so jaded." She reached out and grasped Rhiann's hand.

"He shut me out entirely—told me to stay out of his life. Not only that, but he shook my faith in my own abilities. I gave up a job I loved to better be able to avoid him. If I'm jaded, there are plenty of reasons," Rhiann said quietly.

"Well, you met me, though, so that was fate," Charlie argued. "But I'm telling you true: that man might have some hate for you, but there's something far deeper peeking out when he looks at you."

"Listen to an old lady and don't let a chance at love pass you by. You might get burned—but what if you don't?"

Rhiann held the woman's hand, closing her eyes before tears made it to the surface. "I wouldn't even know where to start."

"You have his cell number, right?" Charlie asked.

"Yes..."

"Call him."

The old woman made a tsking sound. "That's a bit forward. Perhaps you could send him one of those little messages on his phone, though. Just something small."

"Oh, yeah, a text might be better," Charlie agreed. "Ask him how his surgery went. How many kids that donor saved. I bet he's found out since you mentioned it."

"I don't know about this..."

Rhiann swallowed hard. Patrick had made his position clear, and while he had shown hints of the friend she'd lost he was still ice-cold in most of their interactions. What if she pushed too far and he refused to help Levi as a result?

"Text him." Charlie's voice got gruff and his words came out like orders. "Go on."

"Yes, dear—go on." The elderly lady smiled at Rhiann. "I insist."

"Peer pressure doesn't end in high school, does it?"

Rhiann pulled her phone out and tapped in a message, asking if Patrick had found out how many lives the donor had saved. Surely such a simple follow-up question wouldn't be too upsetting?

She shoved the phone back into her pocket, her cheeks warming as she blushed. "There. Done. And when he ignores me I'm going to come over and tell you about it."

"I'd love to have you visit—even if it is just to say *I told you so.*"

Rhiann's heart softened at the hope in her patient's voice. She squeezed the elderly woman's hand. "My son has some health issues that make taking him out much a little dangerous right now, so I can't make any promises. But I'll do my best to visit when I can."

Charlie volunteered to visit on occasion too, and they passed the rest of the ride in simple small talk that took some of the pressure off Rhiann.

They'd dropped the patient off and were sitting around at the station house when Patrick's response came.

Six lives saved. Heart, lungs, kidneys to two patients, liver, and pancreas.

She held the phone close to her heart and tried not to tear up. Not just because six lives had changed for the better that day, but for the family whose world was now shattered.

"That your doc?" asked Charlie.

She wiped at her eyes. "I told you before—he's not mine."

"Yet." Charlie winked as he went to clock out. "Keep texting him and he might be."

CHAPTER FOUR

Patrick

PATRICK WAS MID-SHAVE when his phone buzzed. He finished quickly and wiped the last of the shaving cream from his face with a towel. As he was walking through to the bedroom, to get dressed for a long appointment-filled day at the office, he unlocked his phone and checked the incoming message.

He couldn't help but smile as he pulled up a picture of Levi, sleeping peacefully. The smile faded quickly when he read the accompanying caption.

He sleeps. I stay up and worry.

Patrick hit reply, concern for his former best friend bounding up over the ever-present animosity.

How long has it been since you have slept through the night?

He sat on the edge of his bed for several minutes, waiting for a reply that didn't come.

After several minutes had passed, with no response, he finished dressing and packed his laptop and chargers into his bag.

His phone buzzed with Rhiann's reply as he was getting into his car.

Oh, probably not since his birth.

He needs you to take care of yourself properly and that means sleep.

Then fix him for me so I don't have to worry that he won't wake up.

Patrick sank into the leather seat and scrubbed a hand across his face. Even in a text message, her worry for that little boy came through loud and clear. And now he was worrying about *her*. While he'd tried not to see it, tried not to care, he'd noticed she looked like she wasn't sleeping, most likely not eating right either.

Rhiann was putting all her energy into caring for her son, but who was caring for her?

I'll do my best. Heading into the office now. You working today?

Patrick drove to his office, ignoring the buzzing of his phone while the car was moving. As soon as he'd put the car in "park," he snatched up the phone with a speed that would embarrass him when he thought back on it later.

Currently sitting at the station waiting on the guy filling in for Charlie, who is running late. I hate lateness. It's like my biggest pet peeve.

Patrick laughed as he stared down at the screen.

Says the girl who was late to first period at least three days a week in senior year?

You would know. You made me late most of those days.

Patrick grinned down at the phone, remembering back to high school. He had tried so hard to impress Rhiann back then, when he'd been all gangly teenage awkwardness and she had been the most beautiful girl he'd ever seen.

From the day he'd walked into third period Biology, after transferring his freshman year, and the teacher had assigned him to sit next to a tiny blonde with a wide smile that had sent his fourteen-year-old heart into orbit with his first real crush, Rhiann had been the most important person in his life. He had wanted her love almost as much as he'd wanted air to breathe.

It hadn't been meant to be. But their friendship had been his rock for so long. It had got him through his gawky years. It had kept him grounded when he'd finally matured into a frame that had drawn more female attention than he'd known how to handle.

Rhiann had been at his side, laughing at his sad attempts at flirting, turning him down gently when he'd occasionally worked up the courage to ask her out. Each time she'd hug him tight and whisper, "Losing you as my best friend would break me. I could never risk it."

Had the fracturing of their friendship contributed to her current fragile state?

He leaned back against the seat and closed his eyes. Was he partially to blame for the shadows under her eyes and the thinness of her frame?

Despite his mental determination not to care about what happened to her, his heart was not so hardened to her plight. And the fact that he was softening toward her was tearing him up inside. She'd cost him everything. Why couldn't he keep that focus at the front of his mind?

When he replied to her message he kept the tone light, away from the dark depths where his thoughts had gone.

If you were late because of me it's because you distracted me until I couldn't think, woman!

I would never distract anyone! I'm innocent! One hundred percent!

Lies, all lies! I gotta go examine sick kids now. Tell me something funny to distract me from the sad reality of my day.

What he'd told Rhiann was true. His job could be sad. Very sad. All those little ones with hearts that didn't pump properly. Hearts that had holes. Hearts that had just plain failed.

After losing his own daughter, he had put up walls that kept him from caring about another child. He couldn't risk the pain ever again. And he hated it that Levi and Rhiann were finding cracks in those walls.

But at the same time he couldn't bring himself to put the distance back between them. Despite Rhiann's objections, he could have passed

Levi's case over to Clay. He *could* have. Perhaps even *should* have. But he hadn't.

He got out of the car and headed in. The receptionist and office staff were already in. They always got there before he did, to open the office and prep the exam rooms for the day. He waved distractedly at one of his nurses when she greeted him as he walked down the hall to his office. He dropped his bag on the table and went to the break room in search of coffee.

After pouring a cup, he was enjoying the dark brew when his phone buzzed again. He pulled it out of his pocket and nearly choked on the hot liquid when he read Rhiann's words.

Well, we just left the local elementary school, where we had to extract a little guy from a chair. Got a panic call from the teacher. Get there and the little dude is totally chilling, eating a snack one of the other kids got him, while the adults are running in circles around him.

How did he get stuck in a chair?

On his knees in the seat, apparently. Slipped through the hole in the back and couldn't come back through. His belly got stuck.

Wow. That's just...wow.

"And just who are you texting and smiling at so intently this early?" Clay asked, an all-knowing grin on his face.

"An old friend," Patrick said, refusing to give him the satisfaction of admitting that he was texting Rhiann. He shoved his phone in his pocket before Clay could come read over his shoulder.

"Rhiann?"

Patrick lifted one shoulder in what he hoped was a casual non-committal reply.

Clay's grin widened and Patrick tensed up for the teasing that was sure to come. But Clay only shot him a conspiratorial wink before turning his attention to the coffee pot.

Rhiann

Rhiann ran around her apartment, gathering up the items Levi might need at the hospital. The relief paramedic had been twenty minutes late, and now she was going to be cutting it a lot shorter that she'd have liked.

In her head, she checked off the list: Mr. Bunny, extra clothes, diapers, formula, sippy cup. She also tossed in a juice box and some applesauce in case he was hungry. She was hoping that after his surgery formula would be a distant memory, but for now he needed the extra nutrition it provided. The last thing she shoved into the now bulging diaper bag was her purse.

"Come on, little guy!" she said, trying to inject some fake excitement about the day into her exhausted tone. She picked Levi up out of his playpen, where he'd been sitting with some toy blocks and hugged him close. "We're going to visit Patrick again. I'm sad to say you haven't been able to get to know him yet, but I'm hoping that's gonna change. You see, not only is he your doctor, he has been Mommy's best friend for a very long time. We just had a timeout on our friendship. Long story… Maybe I'll tell you sometime."

Juggling Levi and the diaper bag, she managed to lock the apartment door without dropping anything. She slowly made her way down the steep, narrow stairs of her building and out to the parking lot. Tossing the diaper bag onto the backseat, she settled Levi in his car seat and buckled him in safely.

After digging her keys out of the pocket of her jeans, she sank into the driver's seat. When she turned the key in the ignition, though, all she heard was an odd whirring sound and some random clicks. Tears filled her eyes and she pressed her head against the steering wheel.

"Not today, please," she prayed aloud.

Not that any other day would be better. Another car repair was so far from being within her budget that it might as well be on Mars. But Levi couldn't miss this appointment.

"Come on, car. Please be good to me."

She tried the key again.

Nada. Not even the whirring this time.

She slapped her hand against the wheel in frustration, her thoughts churning with questions. Who could she call to get a ride quickly, so they didn't miss the appointment? How could she afford to repair the car? How could she afford *not* to repair the car?

Before she could think it out, she dug her purse out of the diaper bag and got her phone. She dialed Patrick's number, calling on him to rescue her like she'd done a hundred times in their nearly two decades of friendship.

"Hey, are you on your way to the hospital?" Patrick asked when he answered. "I should be there before long myself."

"Any way you could take a detour out to the suburbs?" She paused before explaining her dilemma. "I'm having a bit of car trouble. Okay, more than a bit. It refuses to start."

"Uh…"

He paused, and Rhiann's heart paused along with him. If he said no she'd have to pay for a cab or an Uber that would cost a fortune she didn't have.

"Yeah, I can come pick you up. Text me your address and I'll head that way now."

Rhiann hung up the phone and texted him her address.

Closing her eyes, she let frustrated tears fall for a moment, before wiping her face and taking a deep breath. This broken-down car was *not* going to break her. She'd been through far worse and come out the victor. So, after another minute of self-pity, she pulled herself together— because she would not become one of those weak women she hated, always blubbering and clinging to a man like she couldn't live without him.

She'd been flying solo with Levi for this long without having anyone to lean on. Staying strong was what she did. Her entire career had been built on her ability to stay cool under pressure, so she sure wasn't going to let a broken-down old car crumple her like a tissue.

Exhaling slowly, she pulled her emotions back under tentative control. "You've got this. You always do," she whispered to the red-eyed mommy in the rearview mirror, wishing she could truly believe that.

Her fingers touched on the simple necklace hidden beneath the collar of her shirt, seeking the comfort the little trinket always provided. While she wished someone else could give her the pep talk she desperately needed, as usual she was flying solo, so she had to fuss at her reflection herself.

"You've purged your tears, now Levi needs you to be strong again. You are all he has, and you can't let him down."

She called a mechanic friend who usually cut her a good deal. "Hey, TJ—it's Rhiann. My car is being a punk again. Could you look at it today?"

"Yeah, where's it at?"

"At my apartment."

"I can come get it in about an hour or so?"

"I'll leave the key under the mat."

"Sounds good. I'll see if I can get it going again—but you know that old clunker's not gonna limp along forever?"

"I know, but can you give it some crutches for now, please?"

"I'll try, babe. But it may be tomorrow before I can get it back to you."

"Thanks, TJ." She hung up the phone and leaned back against the headrest. If TJ couldn't fix the car, it couldn't be fixed. And if it couldn't be fixed, that opened up a whole new barrel of stress.

But didn't have time to start worrying about that now. Shaking her head, she fiddled with her keyring until she'd pulled her car key free of the rest. After glancing around the parking lot to see if anyone was watching, and then chastising herself for the silly thought that someone might steal her busted car, she tucked the key under the floor mat.

Unbuckling Levi from his car seat, she sat him on the backseat and gave him a toy to play with from the diaper bag.

"Here—Mommy has to take your seat out of the car so it can go in Patrick's car. I'm not sure what he drives now, but I promise it will be the nicest car you'll have ever ridden in."

Sadness washed over her at that thought. When she'd found out she was pregnant she'd had plans to give Levi the world. She'd failed. Her dreams had been brought down to the simple hope of giving him a future. Any future.

She unclipped the buckles holding his car seat and shook a few crumbs out of it. "There...now we won't mess up Patrick's car." Then she put the seat back in its place. Walking around the car, she climbed into the backseat, picking Levi up and giving him a kiss on the cheek.

Levi smiled, patting her face. "Do 'gain."

Rhiann laughed. "You want more kisses? My little kissy monster!" She gave him several kisses on his face, exaggerating the sounds. "Mwah! Mwah!"

A shiny black sedan pulled into the empty

spot next to them. Rhiann knew without being able to see through the tinted windows that it was Patrick. No one else would be pulling in to this complex in a late-model luxury sedan.

She stepped out of her old clunker with Levi in her arms just as Patrick was getting out of his car.

"Hi. Thanks for this," she said awkwardly.

"You need a better car."

Wrapping Levi in a tight hug—the kind of hug she wished someone would give *her* at the moment—Rhiann responded tightly, "Yeah, well, I need a lot of things. But you know… priorities." Her words held a note of hurt she hoped wouldn't be audible to him, but from his wince she knew it had been.

"That didn't come out as I intended," he offered, his tone apologetic.

"Whatever." Rhiann pointed across the car. "His car seat is just sitting there on the seat. Can you put it in your car? Or would you rather hold him while I do it?"

Patrick glanced toward the seat. "I think it would be faster, and probably safer, if I take him and you put the seat in properly. I'm sure I can do it, but it will take me longer than it would you, for sure. And we're going to be pushing it to make our scheduled appointment time as it is."

He held his hands out to Levi.

"Hey, buddy. Do you remember me? Wanna come hang with me while Mommy gets your seat in my car?"

Levi dove toward Patrick's outstretched arms.

"I'm gonna take that as a yes," Patrick said with a laugh. "How are you this morning? I'm going to look at your heart today—did you know?"

When Patrick bent down to kiss the top of her son's head Rhiann couldn't help her sharp intake of breath. And as their eyes met over Levi's head Patrick smiled at her. Not just any smile—*the* smile. The one that had made many a girl swoon.

Rhiann learned she was far from immune herself as her heart fluttered in major awareness. She'd always found Patrick attractive. She was straight and had perfect vision, after all. And they had tentatively flirted with the idea of dating once upon a time. But they hadn't wanted to ruin their friendship. *She* hadn't wanted to ruin their friendship.

Then Patrick had gone away to medical school. By the time he'd finished he'd met Mallory and Rhiann had met Pete. Their friendship had continued, but any hopes of more had been firmly shelved since they'd both been married to other people.

Those days felt like a lifetime ago.

Now the very thought of anything else between them seemed impossible.

Even if her heart was shouting out *It's possible!* with each and every beat.

Patrick raised a single dark eyebrow and she noticed the mischievous interest in his eyes. His smile widened, and Rhiann's heart stumbled to a stop before jerking into a crazy rhythm that would have made the cardiologist currently in front of her concerned if he'd had her hooked up to an EKG.

"You okay there, Rhiann?" he asked, his low voice rumbling and doing things to her that a simple conversation shouldn't do.

"Fine." She jumped into action, installing the car seat quickly, listening to the one-sided conversation Patrick was having with Levi.

She couldn't help but smile at the tender way Patrick spoke to her son. He paused after his questions to give Levi a chance to answer, even used simple language to help the little one understand him.

The man was born to be a father.

CHAPTER FIVE

Patrick

Having Rhiann in the car so close—close enough to touch—made thoughts run through Patrick's head. And those thoughts troubled him, given his history with Rhiann. But his anger from a few days ago had mellowed into an edgy awareness of her presence. Instead of wanting to ignore her and push her away, he wanted to pull her close and inhale the soft scent that surrounded her.

Merging onto the interstate, he brought the car up to speed quickly.

Rhiann made an appreciative noise from the passenger seat.

"Man, this car is a thing of beauty!" she said, with a wistful-sounding sigh. She ran a hand along the dashboard. "It's *so* much nicer than my plastic-covered non-starter."

Patrick chuckled. "It cost a fair bit more too."

She leaned back into the leather. "I don't think

I've ever ridden in anything this fancy. It puts Ol' Betsy to shame."

When he'd turned sixteen Patrick's parents had bought him a base model sedan with absolutely zero frills, but good gas mileage and safety ratings. Rhiann had affectionately named the boring gray sedan Ol' Betsy, and the name had stuck.

"Ah, but remember the times we used to have in that old car? All the trouble we got into? Ol' Betsy was a solid companion for me all through high school, college, and med school." He changed lanes. "She was a good car. She had over three hundred thousand miles on her when I sold her off."

"If only my clunker was as reliable." She sighed again, and this time the sound was filled with worry, if he wasn't mistaken.

"You used to have a Mustang," he said. "You kept that candy-apple-red shining like a light. What happened to that?"

"Babies with broken hearts are expensive." She shrugged.

"Does your car break down often?"

She huffed out what sounded like an annoyed breath. "More than I care to admit to a man driving a car worth more than I make in a year."

Patrick let the conversation trail off for a moment while he tried to think of a response that wouldn't get her back up. Finally he decided to just change the subject.

"They put Levi's shunt in during a cath, right?"

"Yes."

"Okay—so you're familiar with the procedure, then."

"Somewhat. I know they'll put him to sleep and you'll go in through a vein or an artery in his groin. Last time he was so bruised that he didn't hardly move for days."

"Knowing he bruises easily, I'll do my best to be gentle."

"Okay."

Rhiann grew quiet and stared out the window as cars and the south side of the city flew past. Patrick didn't mind. He let the silence fill the car and drew in a few deep, calming breaths.

He had to get his mind straight for this procedure and not let himself be distracted by his patient's mother. Pushing Rhiann into that role would help him get the mental clarity he needed to treat Levi appropriately.

He pulled into the parking garage at the hospital and parked in the staff parking lot. When Rhiann mentioned being glad he was there so they could walk in together, Patrick realized he needed a little more space between them. He had to get this procedure right.

When they reached the sidewalk, he waved a hand toward the main entrance. "If you and Levi go through those doors, then continue down the hall to the second set of elevators. Take them up to the fifth floor and just follow the signs to the Children's Cardiology Admission Unit. They'll get him checked in and get him prepped."

"You aren't coming in with us?" Rhiann asked, nibbling on her lower lip like she did when she was nervous.

Patrick indicated the staff entrance. "I'll meet you up there. I gotta go this way and get my stuff prepped."

She looked a little teary-eyed for a moment, before squaring her shoulders and nodding at him. Taking Levi from him, she said, "We got this. Right, little guy?"

Unlike the naïve child in her arms, Patrick remained unconvinced. He wavered for a moment about going in with her, but in the end he kept his distance.

He stood on the sidewalk and watched them walk away. *Distance*, he reminded himself.

With a determined attitude, he strode toward the staff entrance and headed up to the CCAU to get prepped for Levi's procedure.

It didn't take him long to change into fresh scrubs and double-check the procedure room. His favorite anesthesiologist was working with him. He nodded at the older man, who was checking his own prep.

Satisfied that everything was to his liking, Patrick made his way out to the holding area, where Rhiann would be waiting with Levi.

She smiled when he walked in, but it didn't reach her eyes. The fear in them cut him deep and he had to force his emotions down again, become the Ice Castle, as the nurses referred to him.

"Has the anesthetist been out to talk to you?" he asked.

"Yes, a little while ago. Are you going to start soon?"

He nodded. "Just waiting on them to get him sedated, then we'll bring him in. I'll come out to talk to you when he's being moved to Recovery."

He turned to walk away, and had almost made a clean getaway when he heard her whisper, "Take care of him, please, Patrick."

He released a ragged breath and kept walking. If he turned around—if he saw the emotion her voice held portrayed on her face—he wasn't sure he would be able to do this procedure and Levi needed him.

The walls he'd built around his heart cracked.

Ice shards as big as daggers stabbed into his chest.

A small voice inside his head whispered that Levi's mommy needed him too.

Walking into the scrub room, he leaned against the wall for a moment. Since Rhiann's return to his life his icy walls of self-protection had started melting away. Powerless to stop the avalanche of painful memories and the emotions they uncovered, Patrick buried his face in his hands.

He shouldn't care about Rhiann, or her emotional state. He shouldn't care how this was affecting her or anything outside of taking care of his patient. Because he'd sworn to hate Rhiann with every ounce of breath in him for the rest of his life.

Rhiann had always been a brilliant paramedic. The skill level she'd shown had often amazed him. He had seen her make saves that he wasn't sure a lot of doctors could have made. And that was why he had found her inaction when Mallory and Everly had needed her so unfathomable.

He could never forgive her for letting them die.

"You okay, there, Dr. Scott?" one of the scrub nurses asked.

He shook himself hard. "Is my patient ready?" he snapped, forcing himself to be the emotionless robot he'd been ever since he'd lost his family.

The hint of concern in the nurse's voice disappeared. "Wheeling him in now."

"I'll get scrubbed and be right in."

Rhiann

Despite knowing the procedure would take at least thirty minutes, at the fifteen-minute mark Rhiann could no longer sit in the stiff uncomfortable chair. She paced the small waiting room from one end to the other and back.

After she'd nearly worn a hole through the flooring, an older woman at one end smiled at her sadly. "First big procedure?"

"Unfortunately, no."

"Ah… I'd say it gets easier, but mine is fourteen, and this is his fourth, and it really doesn't."

"I'm sorry to hear that."

The door opened and Rhiann spun around.

"Patrick!" She rushed over to him, nearly losing her balance when she reached him. She grabbed the door frame to right herself. "Is Levi okay? How did it go? Did you get all the info you needed for his surgery? When can I see him?"

He held up a hand to slow the flood of questions. "Levi's in Recovery. If you'll just breathe for me, I'll try to answer you."

Rhiann forced herself to take a few deep breaths. Her voice was far calmer when she spoke again. "Okay—first, when can I see him?"

"Now, if you stay calm."

His gaze was questioning, but firm. Rhiann knew he'd never let her near his patient if she was going to upset him—even if said patient *was* her son.

She nodded.

"This way."

Patrick stepped back and motioned her into the hall. He directed her with his hand at the small of his back, like he'd done a thousand times before. His strength radiated out, and like a sponge she soaked up every bit that came her way.

Since her divorce Rhiann hadn't cared to date. She'd been asked out a few times, but her focus had always been entirely on Levi. She was determined never to rely on another man after losing the two she'd counted on within such a short space of time. Between Pete's total apathy and abandonment, and Patrick's animosity and anger, she'd decided men weren't worth the trouble. She couldn't count on them being there for her when she needed them. So she refused to need another man, period.

Now, maybe the loneliness was finally getting to her, but her body found being this close to Patrick something she was extremely aware of. And, while maybe she didn't *need* a man, she was certainly finding that parts of her might *want* Patrick. From her hands that itched to reach for him to the nape of her neck that desperately wanted his kiss, and all the way down to her toes that wanted him to make them curl.

"Let me swipe us through this door and we can save a few hundred steps," Patrick said, stopping at a set of double doors marked *Do Not Enter: Staff Only*.

He leaned across her to swipe his ID badge on the sensor. Her quick intake of breath caught his attention and his eyes focused on hers. She worried at her lower lip with her teeth and his gaze dropped to linger on her mouth.

The doors opened slowly and closed just as slowly. Neither of them moved.

Patrick leaned closer and she let her eyes flutter closed, thinking he might kiss her.

The doors creaked opened again, the mechanical sound jarring the intimacy from the moment. He murmured an apology as she opened her eyes.

He led her into a curtained area where Levi lay on a hospital bed, still asleep. A nurse sat on a wheeled stool at the computer next to the monitors at his head. She smiled, then turned her gaze back to the screen.

Rhiann sat gently on the edge of the bed and brushed Levi's hair back. The oxygen he was on had helped ease the blue tint of his lips and hands, but he still looked pale and so very small, lying there in that bed.

"I love you, sweet boy. Mommy's here when you're ready to wake up."

Patrick put a hand on her shoulder. "He should be awake soon. The anesthesia usually wears off in about half an hour, but sometimes it can take a little longer. We'll want him to stay here until he's fully awake and we've seen him drink clear liquids and keep them down."

"So everything went okay?"

"Perfectly. No issues with the procedure at all. I got all the images I needed and he did beautifully. Between the data we got today, and the results of his echo, I was able to confirm a diagnosis of Tetralogy of Fallot and get a better game plan in play for when we do surgery."

"What is that, exactly?"

"Did none of his previous doctors mention Tetralogy of Fallot?"

"No..." She racked her brain, replaying all the conversations she had with doctors, but she was sure she'd have remembered such a term.

"It's one of the most common cyanotic congenital heart diseases, but it's still pretty rare. In the simplest terms, it's four heart defects present at the same time."

"Oh, my—" She broke off, her eyes filling with tears. "Is it…? Can you fix it?"

"Surgery is a definite. That shunt they placed over at St. Thomas was just a stop-gap measure that's not doing nearly enough."

"And there's no chance of it self-correcting? Murmurs can self-correct, right?"

He shook his head at her, his expression softening. "No. It's far more serious than a murmur. Rhiann, he has *four* separate heart abnormalities. He has pulmonary valve stenosis that's reducing blood flow to his lungs. He has a ventricular septal defect reducing how much oxygenated blood his body's receiving. And his aorta is shifted. Those three are making his heart work overtime and thickening his right ventricle. I have to go in and do an intracardiac repair. We're looking at patching the hole between the ventricles and repairing the pulmonary valve, possibly replacing the valve."

Her throat felt tight. It took all she had to choke out a single word. "Prognosis?"

"If he makes it through surgery—excellent. But given Levi's precarious health situation surgery is risky." He squeezed her shoulder, as if to reassure her. "I'm afraid surgery isn't optional, though. If he doesn't have surgery his prognosis is not good at all. So I'll get my office manager to put the surgery approval request in to your insurance company and we'll get it scheduled from there."

"Okay…"

"Do you have any more questions about today or his upcoming surgery?"

She turned slightly, so that she could make eye contact with him. His hand dropped from her shoulder with the movement, making her wish she could rewind and keep the comfort of his touch.

"No. I think knowing all of the details will make it harder on me. I'll agonize over the minutiae and think of every single way something might go wrong and then drive us both crazy about it."

Patrick snorted and an impish grin lit his face. "Like homecoming sophomore year, when you psyched yourself out so badly that you left poor what's-his-face standing on your porch until I got there to calm you down? And then he wanted to fight me for stealing his girl and you punched him in the nose?"

"Shut up."

He laughed. "He told everyone I blacked his eye. Too ashamed to admit that *you'd* done it, I think."

The nurse by the bed tried to cover her snicker, but it didn't quite work. And when Rhiann looked over at her she saw the nurse's lips were turned up in a smile.

"What?" Rhiann asked her curiously.

"I'm sorry. It's just… I've worked in this department for over two years and I had no idea the Ice Castle knew how to smile, let alone laugh."

Rhiann narrowed her eyes at Patrick. "Ice Castle?"

He rolled his eyes. "I don't know what she's on about. I just come to work, do my job, and go home."

"You shut down, didn't you?"

He huffed, a pained expression crossing his face. "I'd lost everything that brought me joy in life. My job was the only thing left to hang on to."

She crossed her arms over her chest and stared him down. "You didn't answer my question."

"And I'm not going to!" he snapped, anger flashing in his eyes. "I'm going to go and check if the images are up. I want to review them one more time while everything is still fresh in my mind."

He hurried out of the curtained area like a pack of rabid dogs were on his heels.

She'd been so focused on what losing Patrick and then Pete had done to *her* life that she hadn't considered what the last few years had been like for Patrick. Yes, she'd lost the two people who'd meant the most to her, but they were both still alive and healthy. Patrick didn't have that comfort, small that it was.

Tears filled her eyes. Her heart hurt for the pain he must have been in. For the caring and loving man she'd once known to have forced all his emotions behind such a cold front, it had to have been bad. A protective measure, no doubt. She wondered how much force it would take to crack that ice, and if she'd ever see her devoted friend again.

"Oh, I didn't mean to upset him," the nurse said with an apologetic tone.

"You didn't. That was all me. Lord knows, I've had a lot of practice." Rhiann shrugged.

She stared out through the slightly open curtain for a moment, hoping Patrick would come back so she could apologize for inserting her foot so far into her mouth they might need to go down to the ED to have it extracted. They'd only just begun patching up the disaster that had once been a beautiful friendship and now she'd had to screw it up before they were remotely close to stable.

But as Levi started to stir, Rhiann shifted from concerned friend to worried mommy.

Once he was good and awake the nurse

brought in a small cup of juice, and then stepped away to check on another patient. Rhiann fawned over her son, praising each sip of juice he took and every smile that crossed his lips.

"You'd think he'd just won the Nobel Peace Prize instead of drunk some juice from a sippy cup," a gruff masculine voice said from behind her.

"I think drinking juice should be a sport at the next Olympics," Rhiann said, a slight smile on her lips.

"I'm sure our Levi will take the gold, then."

Our Levi...

Rhiann's eyes teared up and she blinked them away quickly. She doubted Patrick had meant to claim Levi in the way her stupid, stubborn, hopeful heart had taken that statement. Levi's own father had even stopped referring to him as his son once the words "heart problem" had crossed that first doctor's lips.

Our Levi...

Those two little words made her want things. Impossible things.

CHAPTER SIX

Patrick

UNSURE IF HE should apologize for overreacting, or just keep his mouth shut and pretend the little spat hadn't happened, Patrick stood just inside the recovery area nervously.

That was not a normal emotion for him.

Nervousness.

Scratching at his chin, he realized it wasn't just nervousness that wasn't normal for him. He'd hidden the hurt, hidden the pain, behind the venom in his voice and the frigid mask he donned each morning to block out all the emotions he couldn't bear, and he had been doing it for so long that all emotions felt foreign—too remote to be his own.

He couldn't remember the last time he'd felt anything but focused on his work prior to Rhiann showing up and ripping the stitches out of his hastily patched-up emotional state. Since her reappearance his internal monitors were going haywire. Not only had his blood pressure sky-rocketed, but his heart sputtered and raced alternately, depending on her proximity. And he'd never considered himself an angry sort of man, prone to outbursts, but the anger he now hemorrhaged at the slightest provocation startled him.

He'd left and gone to change back into his street clothes to give himself time to cool off. When that hadn't been quite enough he'd gone to the staff break room for a while and stared out the window looking over the hospital parking garage. He'd watched people trekking in and out, in and out…

Like looking at the painting in his office, finding something to focus on had helped him calm himself. With time and space to breathe, he'd realized Rhiann's words had been uttered out of concern for him, not nosiness or anger. And he'd responded like a jerk.

That was becoming the norm for him when he was with her.

But he'd watched the gentle way she cared for her son and felt an intense longing rise up within him. The love she showed for her baby made Patrick's heart hurt.

He wanted to experience that.

The all-consuming love of a parent for their child.

The day Mallory had told him she was pregnant had been one of the best days of his life. He'd wanted Everly more than anything from the moment he'd known of her existence. He'd longed to be a dad.

But that opportunity had been ripped away from him. And he needed to remember whose fault that was. Why was he having such a hard time remembering that?

"Dr. Scott? I think we can go ahead and discharge this patient if you are ready to sign off?" A nurse interrupted his bumpy trip down bad memory lane.

"Yeah, absolutely."

He moved to the computer terminal and put in his log-on credentials. With a few clicks Levi's discharge orders were complete, ready for the nurse to implement.

"I'll be right back with his paperwork." The nurse left the little room, pulling the curtain closed behind her.

Patrick stood there silently, undecided on how to proceed. The rattle of a bed being rolled down the hall and the incoherent chatter of nurses and patients kept silence from overwhelming the small recovery area, but the only noise in Levi's room was the soft beep of the heart monitor and the occasional glug of juice from the sippy cup.

Rhiann and Levi both sat quietly.

"I'm sorry I pushed you too far earlier," Rhiann whispered.

The softness in her eyes spoke of sadness and regret and he was glad she'd spoken first.

"I may have overreacted." Patrick stepped close to her, taking her hand in his. "Truce?"

"Anytime."

The smile on her face sent his heart-rate up to a faster pace. He dropped her hand and stepped back, pretending to look at something on the computer he knew he'd already logged out of. Rhiann and Levi were getting under his skin and he couldn't allow that to happen.

He'd put some physical space between them and now he turned the conversation from emotional to logistical. "You ready to get this boy home?"

"Yes, please. But…um…" Rhiann winced as they made eye contact.

He lifted an eyebrow in question.

"Do you think we could stop by the grocery store on the way home? My car isn't going to be ready until tomorrow and I could really use some food."

More time with this woman who made him emotionally unstable and her sweet son who was slowly but surely cementing a place in his heart?

Why not? No way could that go wrong.

Saying no to letting her buy food coupled with

the apologetic look on her face would move him into that class of men who kicked puppies for fun, so what else could he say but, "No problem."

The nurse came back with a few forms for Rhiann to sign and some discharge instructions. While they went over them Patrick played peek-a-boo with Levi, to give Rhiann time to take care of the paperwork.

The adorable baby clearly thought it was hilarious whenever Patrick reappeared, even if he'd only hidden behind his hands. And even though he was getting attached to Levi, and he knew that was a bad idea—boy, did he know— he couldn't resist the baby's sweet smile and rare giggle.

When the paperwork was finished, leaving them free to go, Rhiann picked Levi up and he immediately reached for Patrick instead.

Patrick caught him as he leaped from Rhiann's arms toward him. "You want me to carry you outta here?" He chuckled as Levi babbled at him. "I know—us guys have to stick together. Besides, there's a much better view from way up here, huh?" he teased, knowing Rhiann would take the bait.

"Are you calling me short?"

"Is your mommy short?" He tickled Levi's side. When Levi made a happy sound, Patrick pretended the baby had spoken. "No? Mommy's not short? She's just vertically challenged? Okay, maybe you're right."

"Ha-ha." Rhiann stalked out of the recovery room.

"Think we should tell her she's going the wrong way?"

Rhiann spun and headed back in their direction. "Lead the way, then, Dr. Thinks-He's-Funny."

Carrying Levi, Patrick walked toward the elevators.

Rhiann followed along beside him.

Somehow it felt right having her at his side. Despite the past—or maybe even because of it—Rhiann just fit. But wasn't that just like history, to haunt a man with the memory of things he couldn't have, things he *shouldn't* have? It liked to jump in when least expected and parade out the memories. Then the heartache mixed with just enough of the good times tempted and teased him into wanting the impossible.

He tucked Levi into his car seat, making sure his restraints were buckled carefully. After climbing in to the driver's seat next to Rhiann, he finally made eye contact with her. And then he couldn't look away, even though he knew his eyes were probably giving all his thoughts away to this woman who'd watched him grow from awkward teen to confident doctor.

Her eyes widened as they stared at each other, not speaking...

Rhiann

A horn blared on the level above them, and Patrick jerked his eyes away from hers and threw the car in reverse. He maneuvered the sleek sedan out of the garage without glancing in her direction again.

Wariness filled her, and she was uncertain of his current mindset. Despite that, she would have sworn that he'd been about to kiss her. *Again.* Because she'd felt the same tension, seen the same look in his eyes, outside the recovery room earlier.

But learning how he kissed had been removed from today's agenda, it seemed. She sank back into the soft leather seat with a sigh of disappointment.

Patrick shifted at the sound, but didn't speak.

When they got off at the exit closest to her apartment, she asked again, "Are you sure you don't mind if we stop at the grocery store?" She hated to push her luck with him when they were finally speaking again. But she really needed him to stop for groceries. "If not, my dinner options for the night will probably be plain ol' mac and powdered cheese."

Not her favorite, but that was about all that was left in the cabinets.

Patrick eased the car into a space at the grocery store. His shiny sedan looked out of place next to the dull faded red farm truck he'd parked next to.

He was unbuckling Levi before she could get her thoughts straight.

"You don't have to go in with me," she tried to offer. "You and Levi could wait here. I only need a few things."

She would prefer for them to wait in the car so that she could get the things on her list without the distraction the two of them combined would provide.

"Nah." Patrick smiled. "He and I could use a little exercise—right, buddy?"

Levi held his arms out to Patrick to be picked up.

Rhiann shook her head and walked into the store. She got a cart and tried to take Levi from Patrick, intending to put him in the seat. But Levi refused, clinging to Patrick like he might disappear forever.

"I don't mind carrying him." Patrick stepped past the line of carts with Levi in his arms. "Get what you need. We'll stay close."

Her little boy was soaking up all the positive male attention. It hurt her heart to think about how Levi would react when he wasn't seeing Patrick again, and she sincerely hoped that Patrick wouldn't push Levi away once he'd completed the surgery. If he did, Levi's physically broken heart might be emotionally broken.

She'd have to talk to Patrick. Maybe she could convince him to ease his way out of Levi's life after the surgery, rather than figuratively slamming a door in his face. Was asking him to take her to their appointments and shopping like this going to make it harder on Levi in the future?

She bit her lower lip and mulled that over. The Patrick she'd known and loved for years wouldn't have thought twice about helping out a friend, but he'd made it crystal-clear that they weren't friends and he wasn't that man anymore.

So why did he seem to be enjoying himself so much?

Deciding it might be best not to take up too much of Patrick's time, Rhiann tried to hurry through her shopping.

She grabbed a couple packages of meat that were on sale while Patrick made animal sounds at Levi, who tried his best to imitate him. The tiny little moos made her smile. Then she picked up some potatoes and a few other fresh veggies as Patrick touched Levi's hand to some of the produce, letting him feel the differences in texture and describing them to the very interested toddler.

Levi had never shown such interest in fruit and vegetables for her, and yet jealousy didn't factor in to her emotions at all as she watched how carefully Levi reached out and touched a kiwi.

When they moved on, and Patrick told Levi how awesome he was, and how he was way cuter than any of the babies pictured on the formula cans in front of them, Rhiann fought back tears at how amazing Patrick was being with her son.

Patrick and Levi trailed along behind her as she got in line and unloaded her items onto the belt. With heat flooding her cheeks, she dug a little stack of coupons out of her wallet and double-checked which ones she could use today. After matching them up, she tucked the others safely back into her wallet.

Her pride might be dinged by using her coupons in front of Patrick, but the five bucks she'd save would feed her and Levi for a day. When putting food on the table was a struggle, hunger beat pride any day.

She watched the screen as the teenaged cashier swiped each item across the scanner, wincing when the beeping stopped and the total glared at her in neon green glory. Even with coupons, and what little she had in her bank account right now, she was going to be hard-pressed to pay off the car repairs that she'd already authorized.

She sighed and thought about putting a few things back, but she and Levi had to eat.

"Rhiann, if you need—"

"Shh…" She waved a dismissive hand at Patrick.

She might have had to ask him for a ride, but she would *not* let him offer her money. The heat on her cheeks was enough to fry an egg, but she would not let him pay for her groceries. She still had a few tendrils of pride left unbroken in her.

She swiped her card and pushed in her pin number without making eye contact with the pimpled cashier or with Patrick. She bagged her purchases before the teenager could begin, placing them in the cart herself. Without a word, she hurried out to Patrick's car and waited for him and Levi to catch up so that she could load the groceries onto the backseat next to Levi.

She'd thought having to go to Patrick and beg him to help her son would be the hardest thing for her to do outside of actually letting her child be cut open, but having Patrick know just how far she'd fallen in a few short years might actually be worse.

She swiped at the hot tears leaking freely from her eyes while she waited.

The lock beeped and she grabbed for the door handle blindly. She had the few bags loaded and had returned the cart before Patrick had even gotten Levi buckled in. Sinking down into the passenger seat, she tried to wipe the remnants of her tears from her face before Patrick got into the car.

When he shut his door and looked at her, she cut him off before he could speak. "Things are just really tight with the car repairs and all Levi's medical expenses. Okay? And that's all I have to say about it."

CHAPTER SEVEN

Patrick

EMBARRASSED TENSION ROLLED off Rhiann in palpable waves. She had always been a proud and independent person, and her financial situation had to be eating at her. He wanted to help, but wasn't sure she'd let him. She'd grown up with very little and had always been self-conscious about the fact. He couldn't imagine she had changed after being completely on her own for some time now.

After seeing what little groceries she'd bought, and how concerned she seemed over money, Patrick started to calculate potential ways to help her without it seeming like a handout or an insult.

He swung into the parking lot of a local restaurant. "I'm going to grab some dinner to go. What do you want?"

"I can't afford to eat here." Her words came out as a low whisper.

"Not what I asked."

"Just get yourself something. I'm all set."

She waved toward the three bags of groceries on the backseat, half of which were filled with food for Levi. Her gaze dropped to her hands and she picked at a ragged cuticle rather than look at him.

"Suit yourself."

He left the car running and went inside to order some takeout. After a rushed glance at the menu, he ordered what he wanted and two more full meals of things he remembered that Rhiann had used to like, plus a trio of desserts as well. By ordering a third meal he could make sure she'd have a solid meal tonight and leftovers for the next day too.

When he returned to the car with the large bag of food she gave him a pained look. "Patrick—"

"I don't want to eat alone," he interrupted when he saw her pride stepping up to refuse the meal, playing it like she would be doing him a favor by eating with him.

It wasn't a total lie. He'd eaten alone for most of the last three years, and even though his determination was to keep people at arm's length he still got tired of his own company.

"Do you ever just miss having someone to sit across the table with while you eat? Or to sit on the other end of the couch while you watch TV?"

"Yes…" Again, her voice was barely more than a whisper.

"Me too. Let me eat dinner with you and Levi tonight. Please?"

From the silence in the car, he worried she might still refuse him, but finally she nodded and he released a cautiously held breath. Somehow getting a good meal inside her had become vital to his existence.

That realization disturbed him, though, and he spent the remainder of the drive to her apartment complex contemplating how he could care so much for her well-being when he was still determined never to forgive her.

A few minutes later, he pulled the car into the space where her car had sat that morning and turned the engine off. "If you want to take Levi, I think I can handle all the food," he suggested. "Then we only have to make the one trip."

"You would literally dislocate every bone in your arms before you'd make a second trip with groceries, wouldn't you?" she asked with the hint of a smile.

He winked at her, exaggerating the facial movement. "I'd have to turn in my man card if I didn't."

A small chuckle escaped her. "Fine. I suppose I'll carry my son—even though he has clearly decided that you are way cooler than I am."

"Well, we established years ago that I am, in fact, the coolest and you are just chopped liver." He grabbed up her groceries in one hand and the takeout he'd purchased in the other. "Now, lead the way before my arms actually fall off. I'm a surgeon, woman, I need these hands."

He followed her up a set of metal stairs in a breezeway that had more than a few patches of rust. With his gaze soaking up the general unkempt nature of the building he almost walked into her when she stopped at the top of the first flight to unlock a door.

"This is us."

Something in her tone told him to tread carefully.

She stepped inside and put Levi down in a playpen that sat along the back wall. "Home sweet home."

"It's...cozy."

Other words to describe the rundown apartment that wouldn't come across as an insult were few. *Cozy* had been the best he could come up with.

She wrapped her arms around herself and he could see her hackles rising in defense of the home she'd made since being on her own.

"It's warm and dry, and it provides everything we need."

"Did Pete take everything in the divorce?"

The question slipped past his lips before he could censor it. Emphasis on the *everything*.

He eyed the threadbare couch next to him. Besides that and a tiny television mounted on a small stand the living room was bare. In the small dining area a rickety-looking table was pushed back against the wall, with two mismatched chairs and a highchair off to one side. Only a few pictures of Levi in cheap frames decorated the beige blandness of the walls.

"He took all the things his family had bought us, and well..." Her words trailed off and she waved a hand around the apartment. "There wasn't a lot left."

"He got everything and you got Levi?"

A slight nod was her only answer. "You can put the food down on the table. I have to put the groceries away. Do you want plates or do you just want to eat out of the containers?"

"Containers is fine with me. No use in dirtying up extra dishes."

She put the meat and veggies she'd bought in the fridge while he watched over her shoulder. The kitchen held only a few cabinets, and he wondered if they were as sparsely filled as that refrigerator.

Her lips turned up in a shy, embarrassed sort of grimace that he thought was meant to be a smile.

"I'm afraid all I can offer you as far as drinks go is water or coffee. I wasn't prepared for guests."

She wasn't prepared for *guests*?

If he hadn't thought she'd boot him out the door, he'd argue that she wasn't prepared for *life* right now.

"Water's fine," was what he said instead.

She poured two glasses from a pitcher she pulled from the fridge. "No ice maker, but this has been in the fridge all day so it should be nice and cold."

"Thanks." He took one of the glasses. "I got ribs, a steak, and some chicken tenders. Your choice."

Shaking her head, she argued, "You paid— your choice."

He raised an eyebrow at her and waited.

Finally she huffed, "Fine. If you don't mind, I'd really like the steak."

He pushed the container with the steak in her direction and took the ribs for himself, thinking the chicken tenders would reheat better for her the next day.

She put Levi in his highchair next to the table and gave him some of the mashed potatoes from her meal, along with a jar of diced chicken baby food that she'd warmed for him. The child picked at the food, barely eating.

Rhiann, however, devoured hers. She polished off the steak and both sides before Patrick had even eaten a third of his. He put some of his ribs and a baked sweet potato he had yet to touch onto her makeshift plate.

"I can't eat yours too," she argued, eyeing the ribs with interest.

"Please, go ahead. I'm not going to finish them," he lied, knowing he'd have to get himself something else later, or make a sandwich when he got home.

"If you're sure..." She picked up a rib and moaned at the first bite. "These are *so* good. How can you not want to eat them all?"

She had a smear of sauce next to her lip, and without thinking Patrick leaned forward to wipe it away. Her quick intake of breath and the way her eyes darted to his, sparkling with interest, told him everything he hadn't known he needed to know.

If he could get over the past he could finally get out of the friend zone with Rhiann.

Rhiann

Rhiann's heart pounded as Patrick rubbed his thumb along the corner of her mouth. For a moment she was transported back more than a decade, to a time when Patrick Scott had been her everything. It hadn't always been easy, but their friendship had been the most stable relationship she'd ever had in her life.

She'd told Patrick for years that she wasn't interested in dating him, but it had been a lie. It hadn't been a lack of interest. It had been the fear that she'd lose him. So she'd hidden her feelings behind jokes and even pushed him toward other girls—because having him as a friend was better than losing him if things went sideways.

But now every speck of interest she'd suppressed throughout the years was returning full-force. And while she knew she should look away, she seemed physically incapable of the task.

Levi slapped a hand in his mashed potatoes and white mush went everywhere. His peals of giggles and the now cold potatoes clinging to her nose jarred Rhiann out of her trance.

Rhiann moved away from Patrick's touch and grabbed a kitchen towel to wipe the potatoes from her face and then from Levi's fingers. "You think that's funny, do you?" she teased, wiping his little hands clean of the mess from his food experiment.

Levi had saved them from making a mistake. Even if she wanted Patrick to kiss her with every ounce of her being, she needed him to forgive her before they could consider any sort of relationship going forward. They were barely friends at the moment, and their platform was not stable enough to build any sort of future on.

"So…should I go?" Patrick tossed his empty takeout container in the trash before sticking the meal they hadn't touched in the fridge.

She smiled at him, glancing up at him through her lashes. Once she'd have boldly claimed the rest of his evening, but now an invisible hand squeezed her windpipe and her voice squeaked when she answered.

"I'd like it if you stayed. I've really missed my friend."

He shifted back a step, immediately throwing those walls back up between them. *One step forward, two steps back.* He visibly drew back into himself, like a turtle going into its shell.

Suddenly her heart began to race. Was she moving too far, too fast? She'd only just gotten Patrick back into her life, and their brief moments of contact highlighted how much her life had gone downhill since their falling out.

"It's okay if you don't want to stay," she added quickly. Not wanting to push. Not wanting to be rejected again.

She chewed her lower lip and hugged herself uncertainly. So her life hadn't gone exactly as she'd planned? Losing Patrick had certainly fractured her future plans, but she'd survived. Pete's leaving had been another blow. But she was a survivor. She didn't *need* Patrick in her life. Still, if she could prompt a reconciliation by taking things slow then she'd become a snail—because she missed him, and she really did *want* him in her life.

He rubbed the back of his neck. "No, I think I'd like to stay a while. Can I...?"

Waving a hand, he indicated that he wanted to get Levi out of his highchair.

"Go ahead. You can take him in to play and I'll get this cleaned up."

Rhiann took her time cleaning up the remnants of their meal, listening to Patrick's one-sided conversation with Levi. His light-hearted tone made her wistful for long-ago memories.

Leaning a hip against the counter, she smiled as she watched them simply enjoying each other's presence. Levi needed the attention as much as Patrick seemed to need to give it to him. That nurse today had called Patrick "Ice Castle", but there was not even a hint of the coldness it would take to earn such a nickname now, as he played with Levi.

Knowing how far he had shut down pulled the smile from her face. Her heart hurt at the realization that his grief had taken the loving, caring man she'd once known and turned him into a man whose coworkers found him emotionless. Patrick had always had the biggest heart. His capacity for love and compassion had never been surpassed by any other man she knew.

Things had got quiet in the apartment.

Heat flooded her face when she realized Patrick was staring at her.

"Lost in thought?" he teased, his blue eyes sparkling with mirth. "You've been staring a hole straight through the side of my head for the last ten minutes."

Her cheeks burned. "Sorry."

"Why don't you come hang out with us?" He tickled Levi and they both laughed. "I think this little guy might be getting tired of looking at me and would rather look at his pretty mama."

"I don't think he knows I exist when you're around." She moved to sit on the couch next to him and her words just tumbled out, almost by themselves. "Do you think he's getting too attached to you? I don't want him to get hurt when you're out of our lives again."

CHAPTER EIGHT

Patrick

"I'D NEVER HURT LEVI." Patrick bristled at her words. How could she think he'd ever hurt an innocent child?

She reached a hand out and touched his bare arm. The thought that he'd like her to touch more than his arm rose up from deep within him. But he squashed that down to focus on the more pressing concern that she thought he'd hurt Levi.

"I know you'd never *intentionally* hurt him." She let her hand trail down over his wrist to grasp his hand. Squeezing his fingers tightly, she continued, "Think about how he clings to you already. How do you think he's going to feel when you're gone from his life with no warning?"

"Why would I...? Oh."

She was going with the assumption that once he'd operated on Levi they would go back to never speaking again. He couldn't blame her for

Every muscle in his body stiffened at her words.

"What?" Anger rumbled in his voice.

"You heard me." She gave him a sad little smile. "While he said he was on board with IVF, and then using a sperm donor, when it came down to it he really wasn't okay with the idea of raising a child that wasn't biologically his. He wanted a clean break from both of us, and I didn't have the energy for two fights. I chose the fight for my son and that meant letting Pete walk away."

With his fist balled up, Patrick brought his hand to his forehead. If Pete Blackwell had been in the room, he'd have rammed his fist down the loser's throat.

Anger coursed through his entire body.

He'd wanted nothing more than to be a father. *Nothing.* That opportunity had been stolen from him—ripped away in the space of minutes—and Rhiann's ex had thrown his child away like a used tissue.

"We sold the house. There was almost no equity, because we hadn't owned it long enough. I got Levi, my car, and the sadly low balance in our savings account. He got everything else."

"Doesn't sound fair."

She shook her head. "No, a baby with a messed-up heart isn't fair. Losing the most im-

thinking that—not with how he'd treated her the last three years. And, honestly, he hadn't let himself think about what the future might hold for them.

He couldn't—wouldn't—look toward hopes and dreams anymore. Not after learning how badly it hurt to hit the bottom when those plans were yanked away in a moment.

"Who said I'm going anywhere?"

"Have you forgiven me, then?"

The hope in her eyes nearly did him in, and he saw it dashed when he didn't answer her immediately. An apology tugged at his lips but he refused to voice it. Even as they sat there, side by side, hands clasped, forgiveness wasn't something he was ready to consider.

"I see," she whispered, freeing her hand from his.

She stood and picked Levi up.

"It's getting late. I should put him to bed. And I think you should go."

"Rhiann, wait." He tugged her and Levi down next to him on the couch. "I don't want to go back to us not speaking. I don't want the hate that has been festering between us to return. I just—"

"You just still can't forgive me."

The smallness of her voice cut clear down to his soul.

"I'd say I understand, but I don't. Patrick, you're a doctor. You *know* that not everyone can be saved."

"Can we talk about something else?"

Anything else. Anything that didn't make him feel like a complete jerk for not being ready to forgive her. But Rhiann had been in the wrong. He was going above and beyond by even *being* here this evening and giving her a second chance at being in his life after her actions had cost him his wife and daughter.

"Someday we're going to have to talk about it. And we can't move forward until we do. Talk about losing Mallory and Everly."

"I can't talk about them with you. If you'd gotten them to the hospital faster they might have survived—or at least one of them might have survived." He blinked away what felt suspiciously like angry tears. "I just can't. Not now."

A muscle in his jaw twitched and she visibly tensed, waiting for his next words. He closed his eyes and took a deep breath, and he didn't open them until he was calmer.

"Please, let's change the subject. I'm not ready for that discussion. But I promise you I won't just disappear from Levi's life, okay?"

"Okay."

She stayed on the couch next to him, Levi in her arms. He knew not talking about Mallory

and Everly was surely a bullet that they dodged today only to find that tomorrow's ricochet held twice the velocity, but he just wasn't ready to talk about them. Not to her.

"What do you want to talk about, then?"

He could hear the distance in her voice as she pushed him away, probably subconsciously. But if she could bring up the tough subjects, then so could he.

In for a penny...

"How long have you been struggling financially?"

"That's hardly your business." She glared at him, the glisten of tears bright behind the angry front. "We get by just fine."

An eyebrow raised. "Really?" He tapped the arm of the shabby couch. "We had a nicer couch in college. This tattered thing is worn out and probably older than we are."

She shrugged. "It was twenty bucks at a yard sale and better than having no couch."

"Pete really doesn't help you at all?"

Her gaze focused on a loose thread on th couch cushion, her slim fingers following to r over the piece of string like it might answer her.

"He signed over his parental rights an settlement freed him of all obligations to l financial or otherwise."

portant person in my life because of factors out of my control—that's not fair either. Everything else is just reality. I grew up with nothing. We have what we need. I know how to survive on very little."

"Can you tell me what you ever saw in Pete?" He leaned back and studied her face. "I never understood. Was it the whole singer thing?"

Rhiann laughed a little, and looked lost in thought for a moment. When she finally answered her words were measured and the answer seemed practiced, as if she'd justified her choice before.

"We had fun together once. The day I met him was the day after I found out my mom had stage four cancer. You were busy with med school and I was so stressed I could barely take a breath. My work partner at the time insisted I go out with her and some of her friends. We went to a bar where Pete and his band were playing. After his set, he seemed to make it his mission to put a smile on my face." She blinked away tears. "He made me laugh at a time when I desperately needed to."

"And after that?"

"I know you only saw the bad. All the concerts and festivals—all the weekends we went away when he got a gig somewhere that distanced you and me. You hated it when I went away with him, but it kept us connected. It probably kept my marriage together longer. And, to be honest, I didn't see his flaws until we started spending more time apart."

"You didn't see that he was a self-centered jerk who didn't care anything about you unless you were changing yourself to fit the image of what he saw as the perfect wife."

She shrugged. "Maybe I didn't want to see it? Did you ever think about that? No, you just sat there and judged my choices—you with your perfect marriage—while I did my best to ignore the cracks big enough to drive a semi through in mine."

"Rhiann—"

"And now it's my turn to say I don't want to talk about it."

Despite the hurt and pain they'd caused each other, and his deep-seated desire to rub it in by saying that he had warned her about Pete, he couldn't bear to add to her pain tonight by verbalizing his *I told you so*. So he grasped for another topic.

"Levi looks content."

The little one was cuddled up between them, sound asleep, tiny thumb just barely in his mouth.

"He does." She reached over and brushed a lock of hair away from Levi's face. "Sometimes

I feel like I'm missing out with him. I spend so much time at work—just to keep a roof over our heads, to keep up my insurance payments so that I can get his medical needs handled."

"You shouldn't feel bad that you have to work."

"Tell that to my heart."

"Well, you know there's no way I'm going to be charging you for operating on Levi, don't you?"

"What?" She looked astounded. "But I can't accept—"

He cut her off. "I'm doing it for Levi. There will still be plenty of other hospital expenses to pay, so save your money for those."

They just kept on diving back into the deep end, despite his efforts to lighten things up. He decided another change of topic was in order.

"Do you have much of a commute now?"

It was a good forty-minute drive from her apartment to Metro Memorial Hospital. More than he'd want to drive each way on a daily basis. But it was only about twenty to County, where he'd seen her recently.

"Not really." She leaned her head back against the couch, exhaustion lining her features. "The station house I'm working out of is about three blocks east of here."

"When did you leave Metro?"

Pulling one of the throw pillows into her lap, she angled it between them and he recognized the gesture for what it was: a defensive gesture.

"Three years ago."

Guilt crept in—unbidden but somewhat deserved. Three years ago Rhiann had worked for Metro, widely known as having the best private ambulance service in the area. Taking a county job, particularly in a poorer county, had to have meant a cut in pay that she could ill afford to have taken.

But he'd thrown such a fit when Rhiann had showed up at Mallory and Everly's funeral. In the raw freshness of his grief he'd laid out all his accusations against Rhiann very publicly. In front of a lot of Metro Memorial employees he'd put the blame for his wife and daughter's deaths directly on her inaction that day.

Had his words gotten her fired? Or had she chosen to leave on her own from embarrassment?

He rubbed a hand over his face, angry at himself now for the part he'd played in her troubles. She hadn't done enough to save Mallory, but he shouldn't have humiliated her in front of all of their peers.

But in the time it took him to try to come up with some words that might somehow serve as an apology for that, without implying full forgiveness, Rhiann had fallen asleep.

She was curled up on the other side of the couch, and even in sleep her features remained troubled. She didn't have the peaceful look that followed most mothers into sleep. Even in slumber, she couldn't truly rest.

He picked Levi up and carried him into the only bedroom in the apartment, where he found a crib set up next to a full-sized bed and a changing table. Carefully, he laid the baby on the changing table and put a fresh diaper on him. Levi slept through the diaper-change. Then he placed the baby down into the crib without waking him, and covered him with the light blanket he found there.

Returning to the living room, he debated briefly on whether he should let Rhiann sleep there on the couch, but decided she'd rest better in her own bed.

He picked her up carefully, cradling her slight weight close to his chest, and walked back into the bedroom. Laying her gently on the bed, he eased the shoes from her feet and pulled the comforter over her. Bending down, he brushed a soft kiss against her cheek.

"Rest now," he murmured.

Leaving the bedroom, he walked to the kitchen, to make sure Rhiann had put the left-over food away and switched off the lights. Just as he was about to flick the switch, a stack of flyers caught his eye.

He picked up one of the brightly colored pages. The bold letters on the pink paper announced a spaghetti supper at the county station to help cover Levi's medical expenses.

She had to be hating the idea of a fundraiser for their benefit. That her pride was even allowing it told him more about her precarious situation than she'd ever admit…

Walking into his place a little while later, he sank into the plush leather couch and couldn't help but be struck by the differences in this couch and the one in Rhiann's apartment.

Feet propped up, head thrown back, Patrick grew angrier by the moment as he thought about how Pete had left Rhiann with nothing but a sick child and a growing pile of bills.

He moved to the desk and opened his laptop. With only a very small amount of digging, he found the jerk on social media. From his profile picture, it seemed Pete had moved on from Rhiann with a redhead who looked like she'd had more than a little work done.

With a few clicks he pulled up private messaging and fired off a message to Pete, asking for a catch-up and leaving his number in a second message.

Almost immediately, his phone rang.

"What's up, Doc?"

Pete's annoying voice reached through the phone and prodded at Patrick's patience as surely as if he'd been there and poked him in the chest.

Agitated, Patrick paced the length of his house, trying to expel some of the anger.

"Never thought I'd hear from *you* again," Pete continued, without waiting for Patrick to say anything. "Wasn't like we were buddy-buddy on the best of days. So, tell me—why the sudden urge to reconnect?"

"I saw your son today."

Pete snorted. "You must be mistaken. I don't have a son."

"Levi." Patrick's hands fisted at his sides. He was already impatient dealing with this jerk. Man, he wished they were face to face so that he could punch Pete right in the jaw.

"Ah… You mean Rhiann's son."

"*Yours* and Rhiann's."

Pete made a noise of disbelief. "That's where you're wrong. Legally, that kid's not mine."

"How could you just walk out on your wife and kid like that?"

A wry laugh came across the line. "Don't know if you realized it or not, but things were never that good between me and her. D'you have *any* clue how many fights we had over you?"

Patrick ignored the jab. He'd heard jealousy more than once from Rhiann's ex. Pete had never been able to accept the friendship between his wife and Patrick.

"Do you know how much she's struggling right now?"

The line went so silent that Patrick held his phone away from his ear to see if the line had been disconnected.

When he saw it hadn't, he growled, "Hey, I'm talking to you. Do you have *any* idea how much she could use your support? How much Levi could use your support?"

"I told you. I don't have a son."

Patrick sank back down at his desk and picked up the flyer he'd taken from Rhiann's counter. "She's having a fundraiser just to pay his medical expenses. She's barely eating in order to keep your son fed."

"You know what you sound like right now?" said Pete.

The question hung unanswered, dangling between them like a live wire.

Patrick waited for Pete to continue.

The other man made him wait until Patrick was so on edge his knee was bouncing up and down with the effort of restraining himself.

"You sound like a man trying to offload a broken brat just to get between the mother's legs for a night. Trust me—she ain't worth it."

The anger that had been rising up within Patrick came to a boil. He slapped his hand down on the desk. "You listen here—"

"What's the matter, Doc? Can't handle the truth when it's thrown at you? Or did my words hit a little too close to home? You've been angling to get Rhiann beneath you for years—even when she was my wife. Don't think I didn't see the way you looked at her." He snorted. "If you want her now, you're gonna have to accept she comes as a package deal with that sick brat. You're a fancy cardiac surgeon, aren't you? Maybe she'll let you try to fix him? And if you're lucky the boy will die on the table."

Patrick vibrated with anger, knowing that if Pete had been there in front of him he'd have had his hands wrapped around the loser's throat.

"I always knew you had the hots for her. Tell Rhiann *I told you so* from me."

Pete's derisive laughter lingered long after the line had gone dead.

Patrick knew he should have trusted Rhiann when she'd said there was no help to be had from Pete.

And he knew he should have denied always wanting her.

But it would have been a lie.

CHAPTER NINE

Rhiann

WHEN RHIANN LOOKED down at the screen and saw the California number displayed there she did a double-take. She'd taken Pete's number out of her phone, but she still remembered every digit.

"Hello?" she said with caution.

The last time she'd spoken to Pete he'd called to ream her out because the billing department at the hospital had left a message on his number instead of hers.

"I don't appreciate you having your boy-toy fuss at me about that sick little brat you tried to saddle me with," said Pete.

"I have no idea what you are on about."

At least he wasn't going to spend an hour jerking her around before he started in on her this time. Holding the phone against her shoulder, she waited for Pete to continue.

"Mmm-hmm. I bet you don't."

She heard the flick of a lighter and his deep inhale as he took his first drag off a cigarette.

"Your bestie hit me up last night. He's under the mistaken impression I owe you something."

"Who are you…? Wait, do you mean Patrick?"

Patrick had always been a point of contention between them. Pete had been jealous of their friendship from practically day one. If Patrick had contacted Pete, then there was little wonder Pete was upset.

"Who else, honey? I told you all along he was just biding his time and waiting for a chance to get in your pants. Tell Lover Boy to stay out of my face or he won't like the results."

The line went dead.

She closed her eyes and tried to think about what must have happened. Patrick had to have gone straight to call Pete after she'd fallen asleep. The man had some nerve. He really did.

An hour later Rhiann stalked around Metro Memorial, looking for Patrick. His partner, Clay, had told her she could find him doing rounds at the hospital when she'd stormed into his office looking for him.

The elevator slow-climbed up to the pediatric cardiology floor. The doors had barely opened when she shot through them, intent on finding her target. She started down the long beige hallway and spotted him talking to a couple doctors and nurses next to the family waiting area.

When she reached him, she grabbed his arm and turned him in her direction. "How *dare* you?" she growled out. "What were you *thinking*? No, you couldn't have been thinking or you wouldn't have done tit."

He blinked, confusion darkening his expression. "Uh…hi."

"What gave you the right to go behind my back to Pete like that?" The more she thought about it, the angrier she got. Her muscles were taut with adrenaline. Her fingers itched to slap his smug face. "I can't *believe* you would contact him. After everything I told you!"

Clarity lit his eyes. "I can explain."

"There is no explanation! I trusted you and you—"

Words failed her when Patrick pulled her in close to his chest. His arms wrapped around her waist. From thigh to shoulder they were pressed together, and his lips were on hers before she could push him away.

Warm, soft, teasing, his lips covered hers. He rocked his mouth over hers and his tongue licked along her lower lip until he coaxed a gasp from her. When her lips parted beneath his, he slipped his tongue between them and twisted it with hers.

The hand she'd put on his chest to push him back grabbed his lab coat instead, and crumpled it beneath her fingers as she pulled him closer.

A first kiss almost two decades in the making.

It was worth every minute of the delay. Delicious and tempting, making her want it never to end.

Kissing Patrick was awakening sensations that had been missing from her life for a while. She'd barely noticed men since everything in her life had fallen apart, but she was certainly noticing Patrick now.

She'd been so focused on Levi, on just surviving, that she'd barely managed to function. The only thing further from her mind than dating had been falling in love again. But the moment Patrick's lips touched hers she wanted things.

Like promises and forever.

Patrick eased back. When their lips parted they stared at each other, trying to process all the emotion and change that had come with a kiss of that magnitude. His stunned expression told her he was as shocked as she was. He probably hadn't expected everything that kiss had held either.

A snicker from his one of his colleagues startled her out of her reverie after that nearly perfect first kiss. Rhiann remembered not only where they were, but why she was there. The burn of embarrassment flooded into her face and she turned to walk away, mad at herself for responding to his kiss as she had.

"Don't go," said Patrick, his voice barely above a whisper.

He grabbed her hand and tugged her down the hall to an empty conference room. He ushered her inside and closed the door.

Rhiann tried to wrap her mind around what had just happened. Patrick hadn't been supposed to kiss her. That scenario had never come to her when she'd run through the possibilities for this conversation in her mind on the way over.

But when she turned to Patrick he hauled her in close for another kiss. Deeper, more intense than the previous kiss, it made her feel things she'd never felt before. The depth of emotion each of them poured into the embrace was intoxicating when combined. It took all her willpower to push him back.

"Stop—please." She pressed against his chest when he tried to recapture her mouth.

He released her and ran his hands through his hair. "I'm sorry about Pete. I overstepped."

"Yes, you did." Tears filled her eyes. "Then *and* now."

He winced. "I didn't mean—"

"What were you *thinking*? I told you how things were with Pete. I trusted you to leave well enough alone. But of course you always think you know best. And then, when I call you on it, your answer is to *kiss* me? You just told me last night you haven't forgiven me for Mallory and Everly."

"I thought I could convince Pete to step up."

"You thought wrong."

She wrapped her arms around herself, trying to shield herself from the pain that was sure to come. *This* was why she'd been determined to keep men at arm's length after Patrick and Pete had both walked out of her life. Men always hurt her, always let her down. And somehow she'd let Patrick get beneath her defenses and handed him the power to hurt her again.

"Why did you kiss me when you can't forgive me?"

"Rhiann…" He took a step toward her. His hand was gentle when he grasped her arm. "Please let me try to explain."

She moved away, pulling herself from his touch and putting the large conference table between them. "You can explain from over there."

"I'm so confused…" He raked his hands through his hair and looked at her like he expected her to give him some answers.

She had none. "You kissed me because you're confused? About what?"

"Us—this." He waved his hand between them.

"One minute the past is all I can think about, and I hate everything about that day and the part you played in it, but then the next I can't imagine another minute without you and Levi in my life. I'm falling for you—not a teenage crush, like before, but the real kind of love that makes a man stupid—and I don't know how to stop it."

Rhiann stared at him for a moment, unsure how he could both insult her and tell her that he was falling for her in the same breath.

She shook her head. "How can you say you're falling in love with me and yet still hate me?"

"The line between hate and love is starting to blur."

With one hand on the doorknob, she turned to Patrick. "I don't have the time or the mental energy for this kind of confusion over another man who doesn't know what he wants. My life is about needs now. Levi's needs. And I need you to respect that. From now on I think it's best if we stick to the professional boundaries between a doctor and the parent of one of his patients."

Her eyes were blurred from tears as she made her way out of the hospital. Of all the outcomes possible today, the one thing she'd never considered was that Patrick would tell her he loved her and hated her at the same time.

He'd never forgive her for the loss of his family and she'd been stupid to think otherwise.

There would be no promises from him, no genuine declarations of love.

And certainly no forever.

Patrick

Patrick was watching the video file of Levi's echo again when his mom burst into his office, the door slamming hard enough against the wall that all the framed awards and diplomas rattled. She held a sheet of hot pink paper in her manicured hand.

"Why didn't you tell me about this?"

She slapped the paper down on the desk in front of him, the ice in her tone rivaling anything he could have managed.

"Rhiann's son has a heart problem? That's bad enough. And they're having a fundraiser set up for him and you don't *tell* me? No, I had to hear it from Clay. *Clay!*"

He sighed and closed his computer, knowing this was not going to be a quick visit, after which he could get right back to work without losing his train of thought.

"Hello to you too, Mother."

"Don't you 'Mother' me. Why would you not tell me Rhiann needs help? You know how many groups I'm involved in. With only a few phone calls I can make sure this event is a success."

She sank down across from him with a huff. Her disappointment in him seeped from her very pores and filled his office with a cloud of *You should be ashamed of yourself.*

He shrugged. "I didn't think she'd want us there."

"*You* there. You didn't think she'd want *you* there." She raised an eyebrow at him. "The worst thing I've done is allow your grievances to keep me out of her life. I chose your side in the break-up, but I'm starting to think that was a dumb move."

"Excuse me?"

His mother waved a hand at him dismissively. "Now tell me the truth—how sick is her little boy and why is she having to hold a fundraiser?"

"HIPAA laws—"

"I'm not asking for his medical file. I understand you can't give me specifics. But are they raising money to take care of his needs or raising money to bury him?"

"Hopefully to take care of his needs," Patrick allowed himself to answer. He couldn't think of the alternative—not with Levi.

"And the fundraiser is because…?"

She let the question trail off, but he knew she wouldn't leave the topic until he gave her an answer that satisfied her.

"Pete left her high and dry. I don't have all the details. She'd probably be okay if Levi wasn't so seriously sick, but with all his medical bills, and everything associated with that, she's really struggling."

"I see."

His mom's face had tightened with anger. And that was an emotion he could relate to.

"Yeah, I talked to him the other night. He's even more useless than when they were together. I don't know what she ever saw in him."

"She wanted someone who wasn't *you*. She was trying to convince herself that you were not what she wanted. And when you came home from medical school with Mallory in tow, she clung to him, even though she knew he wasn't good for her. Probably tried to convince herself that she loved him too."

Patrick snorted. "I hardly think—"

"Well, I *know* you hardly think—or we wouldn't be sitting here having this discussion. And you've always been blind to that girl's feelings for you."

"She named her son after me. His name's Levi Patrick."

His mother's hand fluttered up to rest over her heart. "Even though you're a first-class doofus? If that doesn't tell you how much you mean to that girl you're a blind idiot—and I'm suing the hospital because you were clearly switched at birth. No son of mine can be that clueless."

"Mom!"

"So she's unattached, you're unattached… seems to me like there's a situation to be rectified there."

His mom's eyes twinkled and she reached over and poked his arm.

"We've had many conversations about that girl. I know you've had feelings for her since high school. And now it's time to put the blame away and move on."

"I think I'm falling in love with her." His voice was barely more than a whisper.

"I've been waiting for you to admit that for years. You sat on a stool at my kitchen island and told me all about that girl long before you even brought her around to meet me. I heard about every shade of blonde in her hair, how her green eyes sparkled, and even how perfect her dimples were. But that was puppy love—the kind no one expects to last."

"How can I love her when to do so tarnishes the memory of Mallory and Everly?"

"Oh, baby!"

His mother moved around the desk and pulled him into her arms. The scent of her perfume wrapped around him, comforting and familiar.

"Of course it doesn't tarnish their memories.

You loved Mallory—and Everly too. I know what their deaths took out of you. But you've grieved their loss and now it's time to move on with your life. Mallory wouldn't want you to be alone forever. She loved you too much for that."

"But Rhiann—"

"So help me—if you try to shove the blame for their deaths on Rhiann again, I'm going to turn you over my knee like an errant toddler."

He swallowed back the protest he'd been about to voice.

She looked down at her watch. "Shoot—I'm going to be late. I don't have much time, so you listen to me and you listen good. That fund-raiser is in three days. *You* are going to escort me there, because your father won't be back from his conference until Sunday morning. And I want you to spend the time between now and then in deep thought about the day we lost Mallory and Everly. Because you haven't been thinking clearly about what happened. Son, I love you, but you're letting your emotions overwhelm the facts. Rhiann loves you too much to have let your family die without doing everything she possibly could have done. And if you really think about it you'll know that I'm right."

She patted him on the cheek and left, her words weighing heavy on his heart.

He knew she was right that Mallory wouldn't

have wanted him to be alone. Mallory had said as much once. But loving Rhiann felt like an insult to his late wife. Rhiann had been the last person to see Mallory alive—the last person she'd spoken with. His pregnant wife had bled out on Rhiann's watch and Rhiann hadn't done enough to save them.

When he'd lost Mallory and Everly he'd shut down his heart. And even if he could find it in himself to forgive Rhiann for not saving them, she had a son—Levi, with his dangerously damaged heart.

He wasn't sure he could risk loving and losing another child.

CHAPTER TEN

Rhiann

THE EVENING OF Levi's fundraiser arrived and not a moment too soon. The day's mail had come, bearing the medical bills for Levi's cardiac catherization, surgical and nursing costs, and the associated lab work. Her insurance only covered so much.

The bills were mounting and so was the stress.

Patrick had already told her he was waiving his fees, for which she could only be incredibly grateful, but the hospital wasn't being quite so generous.

Thinking of Patrick reminded her that he hadn't contacted her in the week since he'd kissed her. Despite telling him to leave her alone, and that she wanted to keep things between them professional, she'd secretly hoped he would call.

Nerves and all-out anxiety swept through Rhiann now, as she hurried around the station, straightening tablecloths and making sure every table had shakers of parmesan, salt and pepper. Specks of sweat dotted her forehead. She pressed a slightly damp palm against the green fabric covering her stomach and tried to calm the churning.

She sighed.

"Chin up, Mama. We got you. I put flyers on every vertical structure between here and the interstate, And Jason covered from the station south, toward the next town."

Charlie pulled her into a big, comforting hug. Life would have been so much simpler if she could have fallen for a man like Charlie. Charlie was everything that Pete hadn't been. Stable, caring, and loyal.

But Charlie's touch made her feel none of the things Patrick's did. He was a good man, but he was missing the kind of connection with her that had the power to shatter her soul.

One of the guys from the ladder truck came in, distracting her from her thoughts.

He whistled. "Whoo-wee. That line goes all the way down the block. I hope y'all have a lot of pasta ready to go. These folks look *hungry*!"

"Down the block?"

"Oh, yeah—clear down to the stop sign." He smiled. "You didn't think no one would come, did you?"

She blinked away tears. "Of course not."

"We take care of our own." Charlie hugged her tight once more. "Now, go open that door and let's make you some money."

Rhiann picked Levi up and hurried over to the door. She propped it open and waved the first batch of people in. There was a donation bucket set just inside the door, with her coworker Jason manning it for safety.

"Thank you all for coming," she said over and over as people started filing in.

She watched as plates of spaghetti and crusty chunks of garlic bread were served and table after table filled up. Still the line continued.

It didn't take long before Jason waved the paramedic captain over to exchange the collection bucket for an empty one. He took it into his office for counting and safekeeping, squeezing her shoulder as he walked past.

Charlie came over to where she stood by the door. He had a wide grin on his face. "We're gonna have to wait for this batch of people to head out before we can let more in. Apparently, we're pushing the fire regulations."

"I can't believe this…" Rhiann said.

And she couldn't. She'd hoped for a good turnout, but the amount of people filling the room was more than she could ever have imagined.

"I told you—we got you."

Charlie winked at her and walked over to a small podium they'd set up.

"Hello, everybody!" His voice carried through the speakers. "To the folks still outside: we'll be getting you in to get your spaghetti as soon as some of these tables free up. We've got more pasta cooking, more garlic bread getting toasted up and browned to absolute perfection, and we have more money to raise for that adorable little boy right there and his super-sweet mama."

He pointed over to Rhiann and Levi.

The crowd broke into applause.

Charlie had to wait for them to simmer down a bit before he could finish his speech. "While most of you are still stuffing your face, maybe someone would like to come up here and tell the rest of us just how much Rhiann means to you personally. I've only known her for a few years myself, but already she's wormed her way right into my heart and I'm not ashamed to say that she's like family."

Rhiann mouthed *I love you*, to her partner. Then she swallowed hard as a line of people made their way up to the podium next to him.

A young woman with an aura of fragility took the microphone. She waved at Rhiann.

"I met Rhiann when I had a car accident two summers ago." Her voice was soft, even with the microphone. "A kid on a skateboard rolled out in front of me over on Sycamore Street and I swerved to miss him and took on a tree instead. She held my hand while we waited for them to come cut me out of my car. I'll never forget her kindness that day. As you might imagine, I was a barrel of nerves, and she kept me from panicking. When I heard her little boy needed surgery, I thought, *This is my chance to come repay her, if only a little bit.*"

A hot tear slipped from Rhiann's eye, burning its way down her cheek. "Thank you…" she murmured, but doubted the woman could hear her over the crowd.

The next to take the podium was an elderly gentleman whose voice wavered when he spoke.

"I'm ashamed to say I wasn't very nice to that young woman over there on the day we met, but I hope she's forgiven me. My late wife had just passed away, and…well, I wasn't handling her loss very well. Losing your best friend after close to sixty years together changes your whole attitude. Anyway, Miss Rhiann came by my place to check on me, because my daughter had called and asked for someone to. But then she came back every night for a week, because she said I was a cantankerous old man and she found me entertaining. Our visits aren't every night anymore, and I don't need them to be, but she gave me a reason to get through the day during a time I had no other reason to. And I want to thank you."

He nodded over at Rhiann.

She blew him a kiss.

Two preteen boys stepped up to the mike next. "Uh… Miss Rhiann saved us last year when we did some things we shouldn't have." One nudged the other. "I *know*," said the one talking, with a glare at his silent friend. "She…uh…she literally saved our lives. We wouldn't be here if it wasn't for her."

She remembered them. They'd been playing with matches and had set something on fire in their closet. One of the boys' shirts had caught alight and she'd put him out before the fire truck had even arrived.

The tables emptied, new people trickled in, and the stories continued—car accidents, home injuries, elderly people who'd taken a fall. All of them had a story to tell. But the ones that touched her the most were those that told a story of despair and how she'd given them hope and brought them back to the light. How she'd bolstered them not just by fixing their physical ailments, but their emotional ones as well.

And, even if they didn't realize it, she knew that was what they were doing for her in return.

Patrick

Patrick and his mom slipped in while Rhiann had her back turned and was talking to someone else. His mom had dropped a folded check in the collection bucket, hiding the amount from easy view, but he was sure it was a nice amount.

He had the distinct impression that any check he put into the donation bin with his name on it would never be cashed, though, so he'd pulled out cash and made his contribution in five crisp hundreds.

The paramedic taking the money had widened his eyes at the amount, grinning when Patrick made the *shh* sign with his finger over his lips.

They grabbed their plates of spaghetti and he guided his mother to a couple empty seats at a table in the back. By the time they'd settled down to eat, the circle of people around Rhiann had grown.

The dress she wore was in an ideal shade for her. Even from across the room he knew it was a perfect match for her emerald-green irises. Her smile was bright and wide, but a hint of tears sparkled in her eyes, visible even from across the large room.

Patrick wanted to take her in his arms and wipe all evidence of tears away. To tell her that a fundraiser wasn't necessary, because he was willing and able to provide for all of Levi's needs. Even if wanting to do that, wanting her and Levi, stabbed like a white-hot knife in betrayal to his wife and daughter.

When Rhiann turned in his direction he lowered his head and avoided her gaze. Twirling spaghetti with a plastic fork, he glanced up quickly to make sure Rhiann wasn't coming over to their table.

"You're trying to avoid her," his mother stated, accusation high in her voice. She swatted his arm and her glare could have boiled water. "John Patrick Scott—what have you done now?"

"Shh…" He took a bite of spaghetti and waved a hand toward the woman currently with the microphone. "I wanna hear this."

"We *will* talk about whatever stupid thing you've done this time."

He was glad he was surrounded by firefighters and paramedics in case his mother decided to act on the anger in her eyes. At least here, if she tried to kill him, someone should have the skill to bring him back.

He lowered his gaze again and pushed the pasta around on his paper plate. But he wasn't really seeing the food. His attention was focused on the outpouring of love surrounding Rhiann.

A steady chain of people were coming through the door, dropping money in the collection bucket and showing how much Rhiann meant to them with their presence. Men, women, even children were walking up to a makeshift podium and saying their piece. Each one shared a personal emotional story of just how much Rhiann had positively affected their very existence.

Rhiann wasn't just someone who flitted briefly into people's lives and then out on the next breeze. She made a difference to them. A life-changing difference.

Patrick listened to memory after memory crossing their lips as they recounted the day when she'd saved a life or rescued a loved one. They spoke of her bravery and compassion. Of her dedication to the job. All of which warred with his three-year belief in her wrongdoing when it came to his own family's tragedy.

Each time someone spoke of how she'd saved them, or their loved ones, his heart squeezed so tight he thought it would never beat again. His lungs couldn't draw air as a young couple showed off a chubby smiling baby whom Rhiann had rescued from choking.

She'd saved so many people in this community.

How could a woman who was so committed to saving strangers have allowed her close friend to die?

The angry burn of tears scorched his eyes.

He pushed the rest of the pasta away. "I need to get out of here."

With one sculpted eyebrow raised, his mother looked him up and down. "Only if you're going to finally get out of your own way when it comes to this girl."

"Do you need a ride or not?" His voice was rough, and harsher than he normally used with her.

She waved him away. "I see several other people that I know here—as you know, I invited several of my groups. And if I can't find a ride, then I'm fully capable of calling my driver. The question is, are *you* safe to drive?"

Standing, he pressed a kiss to the top of his mother's head. Then he did something that he'd rarely ever done in his life. He lied to his mother.

"I'm fine. Text me when you're home safe, please."

But he wasn't fine. Not even close.

Keeping to the edge of the room, he skirted around the crowd of people surrounding Rhiann. This was her night, and he didn't want his presence to spoil any of her fanfare. He stood by the door for a moment and watched as people fawned over her, over Levi.

The line of people coming in had finally tapered off. But the room was full of people who'd come just to show their support for Levi. And for Levi's mama and her contribution to their community.

Why hadn't she been the dedicated paramedic this crowd knew her to be when his wife and daughter had been dying?

His hand was on the door to exit when the paramedic captain stepped up to the podium.

"Since it seems like we're winding down here, I thought maybe you all would like to know how much we've raised tonight for little Levi."

The crowd shouted their agreement and the captain held up a hand, waiting for them to quiet.

"We've raised over ten grand for them tonight so far!"

Tears poured down Rhiann's face and Patrick shoved the door open and stepped out into the crisp night air, unable to stand seeing her tears. The cold seeped into his burning lungs and he fought back the urge to cry, to punch the brick station wall.

The drive home passed in a blur. He couldn't remember getting on or off the interstate, or taking the turns that had brought him home. All he could think about was the relief on Rhiann's face when the total had been announced.

He poured himself a drink and paced around his living room, trying to reconcile the Rhiann he remembered from the past with the Rhiann he blamed for letting his family die. Those stories tonight said she hadn't changed—that she was a consummate heroine who would have done all in her power to save a beloved friend, because she had done no less for hundreds of strangers.

Hating Rhiann for Mallory and Everly's deaths had been the easy part of losing them. He'd placed the culpability squarely on his best friend's petite shoulders, blinded by the rage of his grief.

The ER doc on call had told him that Rhiann and her partner had not gotten Mallory to the hospital in time to save them and he'd refused to hear any details beyond that—hadn't allowed Rhiann even to speak to him about that day, assuming her words would be filled with excuses and apologies.

Blaming her for the loss that had broken his heart into thousands of painful pieces meant he didn't have to blame himself for not being there for them.

The hours on the clock passed from late to early as he paced. Thoughts and emotions coursed through his veins. His heart still ached with the memory of Mallory and his sweet Everly. But when he blinked their faces were replaced in his mind with visions of Rhiann and Levi. And suddenly he needed to know exactly what had happened that day.

His office door slammed back against the wall as he shoved it open. Where had he put that file?

He dug through the desk before looking over to the bookcase. The file from the day Mallory and Everly had died still sat unopened in its manila envelope, where he'd placed it the day he'd moved into this house. He'd taken it from the house he'd shared with Mallory, but had never had the courage to open it and read the medical reports.

When your heart was already shattered, why pick up a fresh shard and stab it through the pieces that remained?

His fingers slid along the back flap of the envelope and broke the seal.

CHAPTER ELEVEN

Patrick

THE TINY DROPS of blood that welled up as the paper sliced into his hand felt appropriate—right—given the pain that lay within this envelope. He deserved to bleed, to ache, as he read about the final moments of Mallory and Everly's lives.

Heart pounding, Patrick pulled the stack of paper out of the envelope and sank down into his desk chair.

A pale pink sticky note rested on the top, with a single sentence written in blue ink in Rhiann's familiar scrawl.

If you need to talk it out, call me.

Patrick took a fortifying breath and pulled the sticky note off. The top cluster of papers was Rhiann's incident report about the call. A form designed to keep emotions out of the mix, it needed facts, not opinions. But a few circular spots on the page where the ink had smeared looked like tear stains.

He swallowed hard at this evidence of Rhiann's emotions still lingering on the pages. Skimming over the boxes listing dates and times, he moved quickly to the second page, where Rhiann's messy handwriting gave details on his wife's last moments of life.

We were called to the scene of a collapsed pregnant woman with heavy bleeding at Opry Mills mall. Per Dispatch, the caller stated the woman said she felt lightheaded and started swaying, then fell to the floor, with bleeding only noticed after she fell. The caller didn't specify the bleeding was vaginal.

As we arrived on scene I recognized the woman as Mallory Scott, whom I knew to be twenty-four weeks pregnant with her first child. Mallory was in and out of consciousness and only vaguely aware of her surroundings.

She struggled to remember my name, despite our long friendship. Cradling her stomach with her hands, she complained it felt like someone was tearing her uterus out. Beyond her description of the pain, she exhibited multiple signs of severe placental abruption and hypovolemia, for which our care directives recommend swift transport to Emergency Obstetrics at MMH.

We got her on the gurney and into the back of the rig. I put in a large-bore IV line and hung a bag of saline and started her on continuous high-flow oxygen while my partner radioed MMH to have OB and PICU on standby for our arrival. I also asked that they page Mallory's husband, Dr. Patrick Scott.

Monitors confirmed active labor contractions with almost no break in spacing. Uterus was tender and rigid upon exam. Visual vaginal inspection showed substantial bleeding. Fetal heartrate undetectable in the field even with multiple attempts.

I raised Mallory's feet and covered her with warming blankets for transport in an attempt to minimize shock.

A major accident on I-65 forced us to backtrack and take an alternative route that added ten minutes to our trip in.

Five minutes out from the hospital, Mallory coded. After lowering her to level I began CPR and continued compressions until we pulled in to MMH.

Hospital staff took over from there.
Notes: BP was one-seventy over one-ten—extremely high. Heart-rate tachycardic in the one-twenties upon pickup.

Patrick shoved the file across the desk, holding a hand over his mouth as he fought back a wave of nausea. Some of the pages flew off the edge and fluttered to the floor.

Three years ago, he hadn't wanted any details. Once he'd heard that doctor say the sentence "The paramedics didn't get here fast enough", he'd refused to listen to another word. He had taken the file, along with the day's medical notes, but had never opened the envelope.

He'd been wallowing not just in grief but in his own guilt.

He'd been away at a medical conference for nearly a week before they'd died. He'd flown in that morning and had gone straight to the office to see patients instead of going home to his pregnant wife. If he'd gone home that morning maybe he would have noticed something. Or at least if he'd been with them he could have used his medical training to stop the bleeding and save even one of them.

He waited until his stomach had calmed some before reaching for the on-call obstetrician's notes.

Patient came in via ambulance and presented with severe placental abruption.

No heartbeat detectable for mother or fetus upon arrival.

Caesarean section performed, but neither mother nor preterm child survived.

Apparent cause of death for mother: severe uterine hemorrhage leading to hypovolemia.

Apparent cause of death for fetus: placental abruption or result of maternal demise.

Patrick's chest shook with every ragged breath he took. A lone tear trekked down his cheek and fell with a plop, landing on the word "demise" and blurring the ink.

The chair beneath him squeaked as he leaned back away from the file. He sat there in silence, letting realizations and emotions roll through his every cell. With every word he'd read, his sorrow had grown. The only way Mallory or Everly would have had a chance at survival would have been if Mallory had collapsed at a hospital. Based on the timeline, though, even that might have been iffy.

Staggering out of his office, he wandered into his bedroom, where he sank onto the bed. For three years, he had held all his grief in, locking it behind a cold façade. He hadn't even seen what a toll that was taking on him until Rhiann had reappeared in his life and her sweet smile had chiseled a hole in his defense.

But now that she'd cracked the ice around his heart, those buried emotions hit Patrick full-force. The grief he'd hidden behind a mask of cold professionalism, the anger held contained by his clipped tone—all of it boiled up and ravaged him.

Waves of anger had him pounding his fists into the mattress, and the grief that followed shattered his heart like glass. But his grief wasn't for his lost wife and child, because time had already dulled that loss. No, this grief was deeper, because it had cut his best friend like a knife, wounding her, someone he'd loved for close to two decades.

All this time he had blamed Rhiann. He'd shut her out of his life and pushed her as far away as possible. But there had truly been nothing she could have done differently. She didn't have the training or the equipment to handle a severe placental abruption in the back of a moving ambulance.

After the way he'd treated her, the blame he'd shoveled onto her unnecessarily, how had she managed to forgive him? Because she had. He'd seen how she looked at him, the hope and the longing hidden behind her lashes and the soft expression on her face when he played with Levi.

And he might have ruined that.

He grabbed the picture of Mallory off the nightstand and started talking.

"You'd be ashamed of me. But it's been so hard without you here. I'm not even sure you'd recognize me now. Some days I look in the mirror and don't recognize myself. I shut out one of the few people who has always been there for me. I blamed Rhiann for taking you and Everly away from me. But I finally see the truth now."

Mallory would have kicked him in the shins for the way he'd treated Rhiann. Never once had she been jealous of the close relationship he and Rhiann had shared. She'd accepted it—no questions asked. And it was one of the reasons he had loved her so much.

Had loved...

The past tense on that thought brought tears to his eyes. But he could no longer live in the past, reminiscing over memories. He'd forgotten how to live when he'd lost his wife and child, but Rhiann had breathed new life into him and he had to move forward.

It was time for him to say goodbye and step into the hope of a future.

To fight for his future if need be.

And the first step in that plan meant he owed one woman an apology.

With one last look, he kissed Mallory's picture and then tucked it away in the drawer. With only the slightest hesitation, he pulled his wedding ring off his finger and placed it gently on top of the photo.

"I'll never stop loving you, Mallory, but I'm ready now to love someone else too. And I think you'd want it that way."

Rhiann

It was three minutes before the start of her shift when Rhiann parked outside the station. It wasn't like her to cut it this close when it came to work.

Charlie raised a brow as she ran past him to clock in. When she got back to the rig he was loading up to prepare for their day.

He gave her a worried glance and asked, "What's wrong with you this bright, shiny morning? Don't you see the colorful blue of the sky filled with white wisps of cloud floating by on the perfect amount of breeze?"

"Levi."

She grabbed her go-pack and started sorting through it to make sure it was stocked up for the day.

"I don't know if he's getting a cold or if his

heart is getting worse. But he just clung to me this morning, and it nearly broke my heart to leave him at home with the babysitter. So, forgive me, but I didn't spend enough time looking at the sky to spout off any poetry about it."

Dread had pulled the sun from her sky and locked it away behind a wall of maternal anxiety. And the only breeze she'd felt had iced her limbs and sent a chill of foreboding down her spine.

"Poor kiddo…"

Charlie slapped a hand on her shoulder and squeezed. He'd lightened the intensity of his touch over the years, thankfully, and no longer made her feel like a nail he was pounding into the floor with his hammer-sized fists.

"We can go check on him on our lunch break if it would make you feel better? I'll let you out and circle around to grab some food while you go in and see him."

"You're the best, Charlie."

"I know." He made a face.

She smiled—her first real smile of the day.

"I met someone last night," Charlie said. "I don't know if it'll go anywhere, but she had me so tongue-tied it's a pure miracle I'm talking today."

Charlie let out a slow whistle. Rhiann knew what he was doing—changing the subject to distract her from worrying about Levi. His efforts had escaped her ponytail before asking, "And do you know who else is confused?"

Charlie propped himself up on one elbow and pointed a single finger at her.

"Got it in one," she said.

"I'm going to let you in on a little secret," said Charlie, and he crooked a finger at her, beckoning her closer. In a stage whisper, he told her, "We men are pathetic, stupid creatures who occasionally manage to hold it together long enough to get one of you lovely women to fall in love with us. If he mentioned the L-word, you aren't out of the game just yet."

"But was I ever really *in* it? I shouldn't even care, as long as he helps Levi, but so help me, I do."

The heaviness of caring for a man who was so ambivalent toward her settled over her like a thick fog, its weight bearing down on her and dulling her reactions. Between that and the crushing urgency of wanting to be with Levi, Rhiann was barely standing.

The radio beeped just then.

"Trust me, if he even *said* the L-word, he's thinking it. Don't give up hope just yet."

Charlie winked at her as he reached for the radio.

were appreciated, even if they wouldn't likely be successful.

"One look had me thinking about futures and finding someone to grow old with."

Charlie was a serial monogamist. He fell in love as fast as most people changed their pants, and out of love again just as fast. He flitted from woman to woman, but somehow always left them with a smile—even when he'd dumped them. Whenever he finally fell for someone for real, she'd be a lucky girl.

"About time," Rhiann teased. "You were starting to look a little old, there all alone."

Charlie just chuckled at her teasing. "I've just told you I've met the potential love of my life—which you laughed at me about, by the way—so when are you going to tell me about what's going on with you and Dr. Silver Temples? Did you hook up last night?"

Rhiann gaped at him. "Why would you think that?"

"He was at the fundraiser, making moon eyes at you from the back of the room. I spent a good fifteen minutes talking to his mother. Lovely lady… I'm sure she made a nice donation."

Her hand froze, the gauze she'd been stuffing into her go-pack dangling in mid-air as she processed his words. Patrick had been there last night? She hadn't seen him. Or his mom.

She would have liked to have caught up with Marilyn. She hadn't seen her in years now. Understandably, Marilyn had sided with Patrick and stayed away after their falling out. But why hadn't they come up and greeted her? Or at least let her know they were there?

"Off in La-La Land, thinking about your dreamy doctor?" asked Charlie.

"More like Confusion County while I try to figure out why he'd come but not let me know he was there. But then again, the last time we spoke…" Rhiann trailed off.

Charlie made a noise of frustration and slammed a hand against the ambulance door. "You can't stop now. You're almost to the good part—I just know it!"

She laughed. Truly, though, she needed someone to confide in—someone who wouldn't be judgmental.

"After Levi's procedure, he drove us home and we hung out for a while."

Charlie waggled his brows at her.

"Not like *that*." She pinched his hand—a sharp, tight pinch to pull his mind out of the gutter. "Purely innocent…not so much as a kiss." She sighed. "But then he left my place determined to call Pete and make him do his share to help with Levi. Financially, if nothing else."

A huff escaped the older man. "Me and this

doctor of yours are going to get along just fine. What have I been saying?"

"Shush."

She didn't want Charlie and Patrick to get it into their heads that they needed to gang up on Pete. She *liked* having him out of her life, and having them pull him back in was not something she had any interest in.

"So, anyway, Pete called me and cursed me out over it. And I went to find Patrick…"

Charlie leaned forward, eyes wide, eager for the next morsel of gossip she might drop for him. "And…?" He waved a hand for her to continue. "Gah—you should write for television, because you are *wicked* at the cliffhangers. Woman, if you don't spill your guts right now, I might have to spill them for you!"

Her sigh was quiet, but weary with the weight of her confession. "He kissed me. Twice."

"Ha!" Charlie jumped up and pumped his fist in the air. "I *knew* it!"

Rhiann shook her head. "But then he told me that he doesn't know if he loves me or hates me and that he's confused."

Charlie flopped dramatically onto the seat with an exaggerated groan of dismay. "Confused? Oh, geez…"

"Exactly." She brushed back a lock

CHAPTER TWELVE

Patrick

Two hours after he woke up, his eyes crusted from the purge of tears and little sleep, he pulled his car to a stop in front of Rhiann's apartment. Her car wasn't in the lot, but for all he knew it could be broken down again. Hopefully she was upstairs, because the conversation they needed to have deserved privacy.

He couldn't be sure she wasn't working today though...

Anxious to see her, he got out and climbed the stairs to her apartment two at a time. His knock was firm, loud, echoing in the quiet of the mid-morning hour.

Shuffling noises came from inside. Someone was home, at least.

Unable to be still, he shifted from one foot to the other while he waited for her to come to the door.

At last the door creaked open.

"Rhiann, I—" He cut himself off abruptly.

Rhiann hadn't answered the door. An older woman peered out. Her hazel eyes narrowed suspiciously at him.

"Can I help you?"

Patrick looked at the door again—yes, it was the right apartment number. "I was looking for Rhiann Masters."

Her eyes traveled his length and calculated his value. Finally she deigned to answer him, once she'd deemed him worthy of an answer. "She's at work. You'll have to come back later."

A soft cry came from inside, and as she turned to look the door opened wider. Over her shoulder, Patrick could see Levi, lying on the couch. The baby's color was ashen and his breathing labored.

Concern washed over Patrick. "How long has Levi been like this?"

The woman stiffened up, clearly taking his words as an accusation. "He was ill when I got here. Rhiann knows that he's getting worse. I'm sure she'll be home soon. She's a good mother."

"I know that." Patrick shouldered past her and crouched down next to Levi. "Hey, little buddy. You look like you feel pretty bad."

Levi raised a hand toward Patrick, but it fell

limply back to the couch. Only the faintest of smiles crossed his lips.

Patrick brushed his hand across the back of Levi's forehead, relieved to feel a normal temperature. He wasn't sure that he could handle the stress of Levi being ill. He tried to stay calm as he mentally calculated all the things that could be causing Levi's decline.

Had he picked up a virus while surrounded by all those people at the fundraiser? Had his tiny ticker reached its predetermined number of ticks?

"Now, see here—!" the older woman began.

Her bony hand dug into Patrick's shoulder like she might be able to physically remove him from the apartment. Patrick would have found it laughable if he hadn't been so worried about Levi.

"I'm his doctor," he said, without sparing her another glance.

Rubbing his hand over his jaw, he cursed himself silently for not bringing his medical bag with him. He'd never imagined he'd need it.

"What?" The woman's hand left his shoulder to flutter in front of her mouth, shaking. "I don't know you… How do I know you're telling me the truth? You could be a serial killer for all I know."

Brushing Levi's hair away from his face, Patrick stared at the baby again. He checked Levi's pulse with his fingertips and wasn't happy with the numbers. Without his equipment he could only go ahead based on visuals. Levi's breathing was ragged, and every breath seemed to be a struggle.

Patrick made a decision, scooping Levi into his arms. "Levi needs to go to the hospital *now*."

"I haven't called his mother yet."

"I understand that. But I also know that every minute we wait could put this baby's life at risk." He stared her down. "So, here's what you do. You call the station house and have Dispatch put you through to his mama. Tell her that I was here and that I've left with Levi to go to the hospital. If she thinks you need to call the cops, you can tell them to find me in the pediatric cardiology department of Metro Memorial Hospital."

"You can't just take him…" Disapproval and a smidgeon of fear darkened her face.

"I can and I will. Now, please gather his things and call his mother."

Patrick cradled Levi to him, the sound of the little one's ragged breathing sending a spike of fear chilling down his spine. The change in breathing when he raised him upright cemented for him the fact that Levi's illness was related to his heart.

He had planned the surgery for next week, but

it wasn't going to be soon enough. Levi needed surgery yesterday. And Patrick could only hope that the baby was strong enough to survive it.

The babysitter stopped arguing and threw some diapers, a change of clothes and some formula packets into the diaper bag.

"Has he eaten today?"

She shook her head. "I couldn't even get him to drink any formula. Rhiann said he'd refused for her too."

"Is there a car seat here?"

She nodded. "I have one in my car that he uses on occasion. It's my grandbaby's, though."

"I'll make sure it gets back to you."

Pulling some keys out of a purse on the table, she walked to the door and leaned out of it. The faintest beep-beep came from the lot below.

"It's in the blue sedan. You'll need to install it yourself, because I haven't got a clue how these fancy new seats go in."

He nodded at her as he picked up the diaper bag. "Call the station and get them to call Rhiann. She needs to meet me at the hospital as soon as she can."

As he carried Levi out the door he heard her on the phone, asking the dispatcher to put her through to Rhiann because of an emergency with her son.

He talked to the baby as he walked down the

stairs. "I hope that call doesn't panic your mama too much, because I think we're all about to have a rough day ahead of us. She needs you to get better. And I'm going to do everything I can to make sure you do."

It took a little maneuvering to get the car seat from the babysitter's car while juggling Levi in his other hand.

"This would be so much easier if you'd let me sit you down—you know that?" he asked Levi while he struggled with the car seat.

But Levi clung to him, and he didn't want to upset the baby when the little guy was already struggling to breathe.

"Here, let me hold him while you get it strapped in."

Patrick looked over his shoulder to see the babysitter, standing next to his car. She carried her purse and had put on a light sweater.

"If you're taking him to the hospital, then I'm going with you."

Levi let the older woman take him, but he whimpered in protest. More time had passed than Patrick was comfortable with while he fought to get the car seat installed correctly in his backseat. He thought about calling an ambulance, but now that he had the seat installed he could probably get him to the hospital just as fast.

He hoped.

While he settled Levi in the car seat, the baby-sitter got into the passenger seat. Clearly she'd meant it when she'd said she was coming along for the ride.

After finally getting Levi buckled in, he brushed his lips over the baby's pale forehead. His words were so low that only Levi could hear him. "You have to be okay. You hear me? I can't bear to lose another child."

Rhiann

Charlie had just pulled the rig away from the ED at County when the radio crackled. Rhiann sighed. That should have been their last call of the morning before they broke for lunch. She was itching to get home and check on Levi. She had a gnawing in her stomach, urging her to get home.

Charlie grabbed the radio after voicing a choice expletive. "What have you got for us, Dispatch?"

"Nothing for you, but I have an urgent message for Rhiann. Mrs. Bradley called to say that a man came by and has insisted on taking Levi. I'm afraid the call cut out after that. We're trying to reach her again and will pass on any info we get."

"Ah, crap…" Charlie fussed.

Rhiann's ability to breathe disappeared with the dispatcher's words. Tears started leaking down her face and she panted for air. *Someone had taken her baby?* The giant lump that rose up in her throat refused to be swallowed.

"Mark us as off the clock, will ya, Dispatch? I'm going to take her straight to her place. She's in no shape to drive." Charlie reached over and squeezed Rhiann's hand. "You all right?"

She shook her head. "Levi…" she managed to gasp on a strangled breath.

Her chest tightened until it felt like Charlie had backed over her chest with the ambulance. Lungs she'd used for years forgot how to breathe.

"I know—and I'm going to get you there as fast as safely possible." He flipped on the blue lights and pulled a U-turn at the intersection. The siren blared over the impossibly loud beat of her heart. "You let me worry about that."

Rhiann wiped the tears from her face, but more kept pouring down. Guilt welled up and threatened to choke her. She shouldn't have left him. She'd known he needed her and still she'd gone to work. What kind of mother left when her sick baby needed her?

In her brain, synapses fired and question after question filled her mind. What if he wasn't okay? What if the last time she saw him was to be him reaching for her and her denying him? Someone had her baby. Who knew what they might do to him? What if she never saw him again? Pete had said he didn't want him, but what if he'd changed his mind because of Patrick's pushing?

She gasped, fighting for air that refused to go into her lungs. "Charlie, I can't breathe. I can't..."

Charlie reached over and pushed her head down between her knees. "You gotta get it together. You are a strong, independent woman. We are about five minutes out and that's all the freaking-out time you get until you have the full details on what's happened. Do you hear me?"

Rhiann mumbled something that must have sounded like an agreement because Charlie continued with his tough love pep talk. Her adrenaline levels surged and her skin crawled with the need to do something, to find her baby. Sweat beaded on her face.

"Levi needs you. You have to be strong for him. Come on and breathe for me. Inhale. There you go. Now, let that breath out and get it to take some of that anxiety with it."

Rhiann kept her head down and focused on breathing and calming her emotions while Charlie drove them toward her apartment. Charlie kept on talking. She focused on the soothing, familiar sound of his voice, trying to keep panic and negative thoughts from taking over her mind and shutting down her body.

Her cell phone rang just then and she pulled it out. "Hello?"

"Hello, Mrs. Masters—this is Jeannine at MMH Pediatric Cardiology. Your son has been admitted here and Dr. Scott has asked if I'd keep trying to reach you. He said he tried to call you a couple times and sent you a few texts as well."

"I'll be there as soon as I can."

Rhiann hung up the phone and opened the missed texts. Patrick had texted her the same information.

"Levi is at Metro Memorial," she told Charlie. "Can you take me there instead?"

If Patrick had taken Levi from Mrs. Bradley and straight to the hospital, without waiting to talk to her first, Levi had to be in really bad shape.

Charlie drove on to Metro Memorial in the ambulance. Even though she knew there was a chance he could get into serious trouble for that, he never once said they should go back to the station for their personal vehicles.

He pulled up in front of the main entrance. "I'm afraid this is as far as I go. I've gotta get this rig back before they fire us both. But I'll check in on you as soon as I can. You're okay?"

She nodded at him and squeezed his hand. "As long as my boy is, I am."

Climbing out of the rig, she made her way into the hospital. She checked at the desk and was given a room number for Levi on the pediatric cardiology floor. The elevator slow-climbed up to the right floor, and it seemed that no matter how many steps she took toward Levi, she couldn't get there.

Finally she made it to the room. She swallowed down the massive lump in her throat and opened the door, beyond afraid of what she'd find on the other side.

The bed was surrounded by an all too familiar oxygen tent. Levi lay sleeping. A heart monitor and other monitors were attached to him, their green data constantly updating on the screens behind him. The beeps and bleeps reassured her that Levi was still alive.

"Rhiann!" Patrick called her name, relief evident in his voice.

"How…? How is he?" Her words stumbled past the sobs coming out of her mouth.

"Oh, Rhiann, my dear." Mrs. Bradley was talking. "I hope I did the right thing by letting this young man bring Levi here. I wanted to call you, but he wouldn't wait."

Rhiann stepped up to Levi's bedside, staring

down at him, seeing how hard he fought for each breath.

"Of course you did the right thing. If Patrick says he needs to be here, then I trust his assessment."

Tears welled up in her eyes and she blinked hard. Angrily, she reminded herself that she'd had her breakdown in the rig and now she had to keep it together. Levi didn't need to wake up to find her flipping out at his bedside. He appeared to be having enough trouble without getting worked up over her being upset.

Patrick laid a hand on her shoulder. "He's struggling. That surgery can't wait. His heart condition has worsened and the time for waiting has passed. If you'll give the authorization, I'd like to do it immediately. As soon as I can get an OR."

All she could do was nod in agreement. It took all her self-control not to cling to Patrick and avail herself of his strength to help her through this.

The police officer in the corner of the room finally spoke up. He had clearly wanted to watch their dynamic and interactions before he decided to speak.

"We got a call from to say that this guy may or may not have abducted this child. What's your relationship to the child?"

"I'm his mother." Her eyes filled with tears as she looked over at her sick baby. "And, no, Patrick didn't abduct him. He's his doctor and he's trying to save him with much-needed surgery." She looked up at Patrick. "Are you really going to do it now?"

Patrick stepped around the bed and pulled her into a hug. "I'll get set up and be back as soon as I have some news." Patrick brushed his lips against her forehead and squeezed her tight before stepping away. He paused at the door. "Now's not the time, but once we get through this crisis, you and I...we need to talk."

She raised a questioning eyebrow at him.

"Not now. First we have to take care of our boy."

He was out the door before she could think of how to respond to that.

"So, I don't think my services are needed here, are they?" The police officer grinned at her. "Finding out my child abduction case was just a doctor who cares too much for his patient has made my day."

Rhiann shook her head. "We're good. You can go."

"Have a good day, then, ma'am. And I'll pray for a full recovery for your little boy."

"If you don't need me to stay, I'll be going now too—if I can get a ride back to get my car."

Mrs. Bradley patted Rhiann's arm and then shuffled out of the room without waiting for Rhiann's reply.

Sinking down into the chair at Levi's side, Rhiann started talking to Levi, even though she knew he was currently asleep. "Mommy is here now, sweetie. You are going to be just fine. Everything is going to be okay, I promise. I know it will be, because Patrick's going to take care of you. He's going to fix you right up so that you can grow up to be big and strong." She wiped a tear from her eye. "I have faith in him. And I have faith in you."

A short while later Patrick came back into the room. He brought several people with him, including several nurses and, most surprisingly, his mother. "We've got an OR ready now. These nurses are going to get Levi prepped for surgery."

The nurses took the oxygen tent away from the bed and focused on getting Levi ready to move him to the operating room. The commotion woke Levi up and he fussed for a moment.

"Can I hold him for just a minute—please?" Rhiann begged.

At Patrick's nod, she picked Levi up for a brief cuddle. Knowing she had to let him go into surgery, and worried that he wouldn't come out, she knew she had to be prepared for the worst and yet not let him see. She blinked away tears as she eased him back down on the hospital bed.

"Mommy loves you so much. You have to go with Patrick now, but I'll be waiting for you when you get back."

Patrick grabbed her hand and held it briefly. "I'll update when I can."

CHAPTER THIRTEEN

Patrick

PATRICK RAN THROUGH the plan in his head, over and over. He controlled his breathing and brought his focus to this procedure only. Everyday stresses and concerns fell away as he breathed deeply. He inhaled and exhaled, clearing his mind as much as he could.

All the obstacles with Rhiann lingered.

Clay walked in, tying his scrub cap. "You know I'm supposed to have a date tonight? With a blonde who has legs that are longer than mine?" He faked a long-suffering sigh as he started scrubbing his hands at the sink next to Patrick. "*And* she's a gymnastics teacher. Do you have any clue how flexible she is?"

Knowing the type of woman Clay usually dated, Patrick had a pretty good idea. "I appreciate you postponing her for me."

"You're gonna owe me big-time for this. I

think first stab at vacation time for the next full year and my next five on-call weekends."

"If that's what it takes," Patrick said dryly, picking up the antimicrobial soap and beginning his scrub.

The scent of the soap wafted up as he started sanitizing his hands.

"Today has been an emotional roller coaster for me," he told his partner. "Last night I finally read through the medical reports from the day Mallory and Everly died. Then I went to talk to Rhiann and found Levi in this condition. I'm already on edge, and this kid has managed to dig his way right through me. I don't know if I can take it if things go south."

Clay considered his words for a moment before speaking, and to Patrick's relief he didn't mention the medical reports and focused on the living child they could save.

"Well, you're probably too close to be one hundred percent objective. In fact, you might want to let me be the lead surgeon on this one. You know I've worked on several TOF cases."

Patrick shook his head. "No, I need to be the one to do this."

Determination filled him like never before. This surgery was something he couldn't pass off to Clay. He hadn't been around when Mallory and Everly had needed him. He'd let them down. But there was no way he was going to let Levi down. He had to do this himself.

Clay nudged him with his shoulder, taking care not to contaminate their scrubs. "And I need to be here to make sure you do. You know I got you, partner."

"Let's do this."

They moved into the surgical suite, where the scrub nurse helped them gown and glove. Levi was already on the table, intubated and still.

Patrick drew himself up momentarily. Seeing Levi spread out, unconscious, looking so tiny and frail, was almost too much. He sucked in a deep breath.

"I can do it," Clay offered again. "Let me help you."

"No." Patrick stepped up to the surgical table. "He's my patient and I've got this. Scalpel."

Patrick hesitated only briefly before slicing through the soft skin on Levi's chest. When he got him open, he found that the ventricular septal defect in Levi's heart was worse than the tests had shown.

"So…is it this little guy that's broken through the ice around your frozen heart or his hot mama that's got you thawing?"

"Shut up, Clay," Patrick growled as he prepared a synthetic patch.

He was getting through this surgery by pretending Levi was just another patient. He didn't need Clay to remind him that one mistake could cost him the child who had come to mean so much to him.

"Ah… I'll take that as both." Clay watched from Patrick's side, ready to step in at the first sign of trouble. "About time you got out of your own way a little bit."

"I mean it, Clay…"

Despite the defect being more difficult than he'd anticipated, and Clay's constant annoying chatter, Patrick was soon able to get the tiny patch in place and thus reroute the blood flow in Levi's heart over to the path that it should have taken from the start. Then he replaced the pulmonary valve that was too small and too delicate to be widened.

"Can someone send an update to his mother to say that things are going well so far?" he murmured, as he remembered what he'd promised Rhiann.

"I will, Dr. Scott." One of the nurses stepped away to make the update.

"You think we need to resect some of the tissue in the right ventricle?" Clay asked. "I think he's got a little too much to return to normal thickness on its own, don't you?"

Patrick nodded, and began the cut to remove the obstructive muscle tissue narrowing the pathway through Levi's right ventricle. After he'd finished that, and carefully checked that the blood would flow out from the left ventricle into the aorta, he closed, doing his best to match up the sides of the incision to minimize scarring.

Some scarring was unavoidable, but Patrick always did what he could to make sure he left as little a reminder as possible. Heart surgery kids had enough on their little plates without adding the self-esteem issues a giant scar might bring.

He took his time scrubbing down. Now that it was over, the emotions he'd suppressed during the lengthy, complex surgery were welling up, and he was struggling to keep his cool. The surgery had gone far more smoothly than he could have even hoped, but Levi still had a long recovery ahead of him.

The baby was weak, despite Patrick's careful management of blood loss, and it was going to be several long days before he could truly relax his guard.

But for now he had to give Rhiann the news that Levi had made it through surgery successfully, and that was something he could smile about.

And he'd go tell her about how well it had gone once he could get his hands to quit shaking…

"I guess you didn't need me after all." Clay looked at the clock.

"I guess not." Patrick dried his hands and leaned against the sink. "Thank you."

Clay shrugged. "That little one's mama is good for you. I'm starting to see hints of the old you peeking out behind the turrets on the ice castle."

With a snort, Patrick shook his head at his partner.

"I'm gonna head out now and see if I can catch a late dinner with Flexible Felicia."

Clay left, in a hurry to get away from the hospital and spend some time with his flavor of the evening. One day Clay might meet someone who would make him settle down, but Patrick had doubts that it would be the gymnast.

After a deep stretch, to try to loosen up the tight muscles in his back, Patrick walked out of the scrub room to find Rhiann.

Rhiann

Pacing from the door to the update board, Rhiann impatiently awaited news on Levi. Each time the board flickered as a case was updated Rhiann and the other anxiously waiting family members would hurry forward to check if it was their loved one with an update.

When the update wasn't for Levi, she continued her agitated strides from one side of the room to the other and back.

The update board listed each person as a case number—nothing identifiable. The assigned numbers sat there on their last update. Some said, "Surgery started" for forty minutes before updating to a "Going as expected." Others flashed more frequently, adding updates that the patient was "Doing well" or "Doing fine." The ones that switched over to "Closing, doing fine" or "In Recovery" earned a relieved gasp or a tearful hug.

When an update finally flashed up saying Levi's surgery was "Going well so far," Rhiann felt sick with relief.

"Honey, why don't you come sit down here with me for just a minute now you've had some news?" Marilyn Scott asked from her chair along the wall nearest the exterior doors. She patted the faded beige seat beside her.

The levels of anxiety building inside her, despite the update, made that an almost impossible task, but nevertheless Rhiann found herself in the seat next to Patrick's mother. The low-backed chair put an instant ache in her back.

She looked around the room at the other seating options. Upright chairs and narrow couches made semi-circles in various configurations around the large waiting room. Along the outer glass wall a series of backless benches rested, keeping the view of the valet stand and parking garage as unobstructed as possible. All were covered in shades of beige or gray. None were comfortable.

"I'm not sure why you're here, but thank you for waiting with me," Rhiann told the older woman.

Some patients had a group of family there, offering their support, taking up more than their share of the waiting room. Most of the pediatric patients had both parents, or a parent and a grandparent. Rhiann had thought she'd be the one sitting alone in a corner somewhere, holding a book she pretended to read. Or pacing back and forth, carrying all her things and the clear plastic drawstring bag full of Levi's clothes because she had no one to watch them if she left them sitting there.

"It's nice not being alone for once. But I'll understand if you need to go."

"I'm here because Patrick asked me to be. Precisely because he didn't think you should be alone." Marilyn patted her hand, shivering when the automatic doors whooshed open and let in a cold breeze.

"We should move away from these doors."

Rhiann didn't want the older woman to come

down with a cold just because she'd been kind enough to keep her from being alone. She pointed to a spot under an arch, across from the surgery information desk. Marilyn nodded and they gathered their things to move over there.

"Why would Patrick do that?" asked Rhiann.

Marilyn settled down on the small couch and sighed when she felt the heat was on. She looked far more comfortable on this side of the room.

"Because you matter to him—don't you realize that?"

Rhiann's heart warmed at the knowledge that Patrick had not only thought of her needs, but acted on them to make sure she had everything. That was the Patrick who had earned the title of her best friend. That was the loving, caring friend she'd been broken-hearted to lose. It was nice to see him starting to be the man she knew him to be again.

Overhead, a creaky male voice announced over the PA system that they were conducting a test on their alert system and for everyone to ignore the incoming message. Despite that, when all the phones in the room rang, or buzzed, everyone looked at their screens hopefully.

A collective sigh echoed in the cavernous space when the words on the screen read, This is a test. Soon, the chatter of voices rose back to pre-announcement levels and settled into a loud and overwhelming din. Nothing distinct.

Returning to her conversation with Patrick's mother, Rhiann tried to rationalize his actions. "We were friends for years. I think having this contact over Levi has made him feel a bit responsible and want to help me. That's all."

Mrs. Scott made a tsking noise with her tongue. "I remember you, and your friendship with Patrick, and his asking me to be here has very little to do with that. This is entirely about my son falling for you and your little boy."

Rhiann blushed at the frankness in the older woman's words. "I'm sure you're mistaken. If Patrick has any emotion for me it's hatred, because I couldn't save his family."

She looked away and watched a window-cleaning crew set up to clean the massive amounts of glass around the waiting room. The crew added a new layer of noise to the already loud room. The buckles on their harnesses clanked. Squeegees squeaked. But even the additional noise couldn't distract her from the uncomfortable encounter she found herself having with Patrick's mother.

Mrs. Scott laid a hand on Rhiann's knee, bringing her back to the conversation she was trying to avoid. "Hmm… I think I know my son better than that. For the record, I never blamed you for Mallory and Everly's deaths. And I told my son he was a moron for doing so."

Rhiann blinked away tears. She couldn't let herself start crying or she might not stop. "I could use some coffee. How about you?"

"I'm fine, dear."

Rhiann hopped up and hurried over to the busy coffee cart next to the surgery information desk. She ordered coffee and a pumpkin muffin, taking her time adding cream and sugar before she made her way back over to Patrick's mom.

She sipped at the coffee and pulled a face as she sat back down. "Ugh. This coffee is almost as bad as the station's sludge."

Mrs. Scott raised an eyebrow. "But they look so busy?"

"Location is everything. And most of their customers are probably patients' family, like me, and don't know any better." She shrugged, taking another sip. "At least the muffin is decent—if a little dry."

"I think my son is falling in love with you."

Heat flamed in Rhiann's cheeks and she dropped her head, wishing she'd taken her hair down from her normal work up-do simply so that she could hide behind its length.

Patrick's mom watched her reaction and smiled. Her voice was softer now, kinder. "And if I'm not mistaken you are feeling the same way about him, aren't you?"

"I—" Rhiann's reply was interrupted by the buzz of the cell phone in her hand. She jumped up as soon as she read the words on the screen.

Please come to the pediatric surgery desk.

When she looked up Patrick stood just beyond the desk, a wide smile lighting his handsome face.

CHAPTER FOURTEEN

Patrick

WHEN HE MADE eye contact with Rhiann and smiled, her face went from anxious to relieved. Then she closed the last few steps between them and launched herself into his arms. Sobbing against his chest, she clung to him, barely staying upright.

"Levi's in Recovery," he said to the top of her head.

He held her close and murmured reassurances in her ear, telling her that the surgery had gone well and Levi was doing fine. The relief pouring off her was palpable, and seeped down deep into his soul. The tautness that had plagued his muscles since he'd walked into Rhiann's apartment so many hours ago and seen Levi in such distress dissipated in the warmth of her embrace.

As a surgeon, he didn't allow himself to dwell on losing his patients. Death was an unfortunate possibility in his line of work, but he didn't like to think about it. It wasn't that thinking of it made the likelihood increase, but there was no point tempting fate, right?

Some patients were harder to heal than others. The more damage he saw on the scans, the more his concern rose. Others he never once imagined he might lose. But each new patient was a fresh start—a chance to shake off any disastrous outcomes that had come before. Not that he had a lot of negative outcomes. He was one of the best pediatric cardiologists in the southeast, and that wasn't an ego thing. He had the success rate to back his claims.

With Levi, though, his nerves had been ragged from the start of surgery. Levi's wellbeing had become critically important to him. The churning in his stomach hadn't eased after closing. The lump in his throat that refused to be swallowed hadn't budged even once Levi had moved to recovery. Only now, when he had Rhiann in his arms, did any of that change.

Pulling her closer, he let his eyes drift shut as a sense of peace washed over him. Her height was perfect for him to rest his cheek on the top of her head. Having Rhiann in his arms shouldn't feel like coming home, like a balm for his discontented heart, but to say it didn't would be lying to himself.

As a teen, he'd wanted to be more than friends with Rhiann, but he couldn't remember ever feeling quite *this* way about her.

That seemed to be his normal lately. Finding new emotions where there had once just been ice. Contentment where there had been only apathy. Tendrils of want replacing sparks of anger. And he was learning to accept that change was inevitable—particularly when it came to his relationship with Rhiann.

His mother came up behind Rhiann, a hopeful smile on her face and questions filling her eyes. "How is he?" she asked.

Still holding Rhiann, because he couldn't seem to let her go, he answered, "Levi's in Recovery. The surgery went well. He's got a long way to go, but he made it through surgery like a champ. The next twenty-four to forty-eight hours will be the biggest mountain he has to climb."

His mother let out a shaky breath. "I'm sure he'll do great with the two of you at his bedside. If he's okay for now, then I'll be back in the morning to check on him. But you call me if you need anything." She reached out and tucked a loose lock of hair away from Rhiann's face with a gentle touch. "Either of you."

Patrick wrapped an arm around his mother and pulled her into a three-way hug with Rhiann. Having a mother like his made him a lucky man.

"Thank you for always coming when I call. I love you, Mom."

She pinched his cheek like he was five and he tried not to squirm. He loved her, despite her determination to make him die of embarrassment.

"That's what us moms do."

With Rhiann still tucked under his arm, he watched as his mother gathered up her things and bustled out of the waiting room with the grace he had always admired about her. She never got flustered, or angry, and he only wished he'd inherited more of her temperament than the more volatile disposition he got from his father.

"So," he said, looking down at the beautiful woman in his arms. He wiped the tears from her face with his thumbs. "Are you ready to see your son?"

Rhiann nodded.

"Then let's go."

Keeping a loose arm around her waist, Patrick led her through the hospital and past a few *Employees Only* signs. Finally he swiped his ID badge at the back door of the recovery room.

Nudging her into the bathroom along the right-hand side, he said, "Go wash your face first. You don't want Levi to see you looking like that."

She brought a hand up to her face. "Is that a subtle way of saying I'm a hot mess?"

"A gorgeous mess." Even the teary streaks marring her cheeks couldn't take anything from her beauty. "I'll be right here."

A few minutes later Rhiann stepped out, her face freshly scrubbed and her hair now loose and tumbling in thick waves around her shoulders.

He pulled her close and brushed his lips against hers, finding comfort in her touch. But it was the wrong place, the wrong time, so he quickly moved away.

"He's right this way."

He engulfed her hand with his own, acutely aware of how much smaller her hand was compared to his. Following his lead, she moved with him through the recovery ward and down to Curtain Five.

"He's still intubated, and I'd like to keep him that way for about twenty-four hours. We don't want him moving too much just yet and undoing all the repairs I just so painstakingly made."

She reached out with a tentative hand and brushed back a lock of Levi's hair. "But he's doing okay?"

"He is doing as well as can be expected, considering how sick he was and how invasive the surgery was."

The last thing he wanted to do was give her false hope. Levi wasn't out of the woods yet. But he was hoping for a good outcome. More than hoping, really.

Because while losing Mallory and Everly had broken him, he knew losing Levi would shatter him beyond repair.

Rhiann

The twenty-four hours following Levi's surgery had passed in a blur. Bleary-eyed and exhausted, Rhiann dozed in the green misery the hospital referred to as "a recliner" in Levi's room. She refused to leave. How could she leave him there all alone?

Levi lay there, looking so small. She watched the machines that documented his bodily functions and could probably have recited each stat by heart. Her little fighter—he wouldn't give up. She wouldn't let him give up. *Couldn't* let him give up.

The nurses came in and out, their faces somber, and Rhiann couldn't help but wonder if they knew something she didn't. But they couldn't comprehend the pain she was suffering, watching Levi go through this ordeal.

The waiting was almost unbearable. Waiting for him to wake up. Waiting for a sign that he was getting better. But the monitors only showed the same numbers they'd shown all day.

When Patrick came in she practically pounced on him, begging him to be honest with her about Levi's condition, worried he was hiding something crucial from her.

He pulled her into his arms and held her close, comforting her with his physical presence. "Like I told you earlier, it's a waiting game now. We just have to wait and see if he's strong enough to pull through."

Patrick did his best to distract her and he even brought her some lunch. "Come on, Rhiann. You have to eat something."

He waved a chicken tender under her nose and she battled back a wave of nausea.

"The hospital food isn't great, but you need something in your stomach."

How could she eat? With her baby lying there in that hospital bed, tubes coming out of his tiny body?

Her stomach roiled with every nibble she took to placate Patrick.

"You'll feel better once you eat," he insisted. "I'll bring some real food in tonight, if you tell me what you want."

All she wanted was for Levi to get better. And Patrick couldn't do any more to help with that.

She ate enough of the chicken he'd brought to get him to hush, but she didn't really have the appetite for any of it. Seeing her eat seemed to chase a few shadows from Patrick's eyes, though, so she was glad she'd eaten if only for that reason.

He sank into a seated position at her feet. "I'm hoping that having him intubated for a day or so will give him time to gain a little strength. Maybe another twelve to twenty-four hours. I don't know yet."

"But the longer he's on the ventilator, the harder it will be for him to come off it, right?"

Patrick reached for her hand and she allowed the touch. "Yes. But don't give up hope. It's not time for that. I promise you, I feel good about his chances."

His fingers were warm on hers and the sensations created when his thumb moved back and forth over her palm provided a much-needed distraction.

"I've missed this," she said softly, not wanting to ruin the intimacy of the moment.

He raised an eyebrow. "Me sitting on the floor, looking up at you?"

"Of course—bow before your queen, peasant."

A snort came in reply.

"I meant us just hanging out together. I hate

the locale and the circumstance, but I've missed *this*."

Leaning forward, he brushed his lips against her wrist. "You know, I think we spent half our free time in high school sitting like this. You perched on one of our beds and me on the floor below you, because if either of our mothers had caught us on a bed together—even fully clothed and obviously studying—they'd have lost their minds."

She laughed. "I know. Remember how my mom freaked out when we fell asleep on the couch, watching one of the *Halloween* movies?"

They spent the next few hours reminiscing, finding contentment in each other's presence.

When it came time for Patrick to leave, Rhiann noticed his hesitation.

"We'll still be here in the morning," she said, and gave him a quick hug.

This time he was quick enough to hug her back.

"I hate leaving you here alone." His arms tightened around her after his whispered admission and his breath ruffled her hair. They stayed like that until his cell phone buzzed with a message about another patient.

"You should go," she murmured against his chest, her cheeks heating at the affection she'd heard in his words.

He cupped her cheek with his hand, tipping her face up so that he could brush his lips over hers.

An uncomfortable laugh broke from her throat. "Are you leaving or not?"

"Not until you give me a proper goodbye." He nuzzled her neck. "When Levi's better, I want to take you on a proper date. Dinner, flowers, dancing—everything."

"Okay…" Rhiann said, her voice soft, barely above a whisper.

Her heart raced as his lips ghosted over hers once more, just teasing her with the promise of what would follow. His tongue licked at her lower lip, delving into her mouth as it opened. But he pulled back before things got too heated, and she sighed at the loss.

"I'll be back first thing in the morning," he promised.

CHAPTER FIFTEEN

Patrick

WHEN HE GOT to the hospital the next day, he was surprised to find that Rhiann wasn't in Levi's room. He checked the bathroom, and the small break room on the floor. The nurses usually let the parents who overnighted with their kids grab coffee there.

No Rhiann.

He stepped out to the nurses' station. "Do you know where Rhiann Masters is? The mother from Room 5102?" he asked the nurse behind the desk.

She jumped when he spoke, and looked up at him with weary eyes. "She said something about needing a shower and clothes that didn't smell like a hospital. I tried to tell her that anything she wears in here will smell like a hospital in about an hour, but she left anyways."

"Okay, thanks."

He resisted the urge to tell the nurse to grab a coffee. Some of them were just not cut out for the overnight shift.

He walked back down the hall and looked in on Levi, who was still intubated under his orders. He tousled Levi's curls gently, whispering to him, "I'm going to go check on my patients, but I'll be back to see you in a bit. I bet your mama beats me back, though."

But an hour later there was still no sign of Rhiann when he returned to Levi's room. "Where is your mama, huh?"

He washed his hands and moved on with his daily exam. Levi was still relying on the ventilator more than he'd have liked, but the baby had responded fairly well to having it turned down slightly. Patrick adjusted the notes to ask for the vent to be reduced a little more every few hours, so they could wean him off the machine—hopefully by the end of the day.

Exam done, he hung his stethoscope around his neck and reached out to touch Levi's tiny hand. "I always tell my patients' parents to talk to their little ones as if they can hear every word when their kids are lying in these beds, so I'm going to take my own advice and talk to you like you can hear me."

He traced his index finger up and down each of Levi's fingers and swallowed down the overwhelming desire to pick the toddler up. Levi needed time to heal, time to recover. Patrick knew the importance of that more than anyone, but he desperately wanted to feel Levi's slight weight against his chest again.

"I need you to listen up, buddy. I know you've had a rough start, what with your bum heart and your deadbeat father. But I'm going to make sure that the rest of your life goes better for you. I've already fixed your heart. You just have to get a little stronger so you can see that."

He took a deep breath and continued speaking earnestly. "And, it might be a little old-fashioned, but I'd like to ask your permission to date your mom. I know we have a past, and you've heard about some of that. But I swear I'll put it behind us."

Patrick paused to wipe a tear from his eye. He'd messed up a lot of things in the past. But he wasn't lying when he said he was putting it all behind him. Mallory and Everly's deaths had started a chain reaction of loss in his life and he was still recovering. But being here felt right.

For three years he'd only existed. He hadn't been living. Then Rhiann and Levi had come into his life. Now, he wanted to be everything for them. He wanted to truly live because of them. *For* them. *With* them.

He cleared his throat and returned to his one-sided conversation.

"But most of all I promise to be the man your mom needs. She won't have to work so hard, because she'll have me to help her with the bills. You'll have a place where you can't hear the neighbors cough because the walls are so thin, and your mom won't skip meals so that you don't go hungry. I'd even like to say she wouldn't have to work, but your mom loves her job and I don't think she'd give it up. I wouldn't ask her to."

He smiled down at Levi.

"And every night I'll help you with your homework. Your mom's rubbish at math, but I can help you with that. I'll be at all your Little League games, academic team meets, chorus concerts… Whatever extra-curriculars you get into I'll be there, because I want to be the dad you deserve."

A sound in the hall caught his attention and he spun around, expecting to see Rhiann standing behind him, listening to every word he'd just said to Levi, but the doorway was empty.

He released a held breath.

"So, you just get through these next few days, and I'll help with all the rest. I have a lot riding on this. Convincing your mama might take some effort, but I'm up for the challenge. What do you think? Do we have a deal?"

Levi couldn't answer, of course. But Patrick liked to think the little boy would be one hundred percent on board with his plans. He took a few deep breaths and a feeling of contentment washed over him now that he'd voiced his intentions.

When Levi clutched his thumb with his little hand, Patrick sighed. "It's all going to work out," he said. "I won't let you down."

Rhiann

Rhiann stood outside Levi's room with a hand over her mouth, trying to contain a sob. Patrick had obviously heard her gasp, but she'd moved to one side before he'd completely turned around.

Her heart had nearly melted when she'd heard his emotional outpouring to Levi. Okay, so Levi was unconscious, and may or may not be able to hear. But it had been a touching display, nonetheless.

Patrick's voice was low now, but it carried out into the hallway. "I won't let you down."

She closed her eyes and made a wish.

Rhiann had never been much for prayer. She put her belief into science and medicine. People. But she had hopes and wishes as much as anyone else. And right now her wish was simple.

She wanted to spend the rest of her life with

the two current occupants of Metro Memorial Hospital's Room 5102.

With a shaky hand, she fished the dandelion necklace Patrick had given her in high school out of her collar and pressed her lips to the small orb for luck. He'd bought her the little trinket at a craft fair they'd attended one weekend on a lark. For sixteen-year-old kids, handmade crafts hadn't been a huge draw, but the shiny resin orb with a dandelion puff in it had caught his eye— because, as he'd said, she was always making wishes, and maybe she just needed a talisman for them to come true.

She'd worn it every day since.

"If you don't marry that man, I will."

Rhiann opened her eyes to see the nurse who'd been with Levi the day of his procedure standing in front of her. Tears had welled up in the other woman's eyes, on the verge of spilling over.

"All this time I thought that man was made of ice—but, oh, my gosh, he's a total softie!"

"Shh…" Rhiann urged. "He'll hear you!"

She grabbed the nurse by the arm and led her away from the open doorway. They went down the hall far enough that Rhiann was sure Patrick wouldn't overhear.

"It's so romantic! Old friends brought back together to save a small child!" The nurse faked a swoon. She even fluttered a hand over her eyes before straightening back up. "All you need is a villain to tear you apart just as he's about to propose and—"

"Hush with all that drama!" Rhiann sighed. "We haven't talked about the future, or what will become of us—if there *is* an us. I can't... My focus has to be on my son right now."

The nurse smiled at her and pulled her in for an impromptu hug. "Your son needs a happy mommy and a sexy new daddy." She waggled her eyebrows. "And if you can't see that man's sex appeal, I'm taking you down to the optical clinic for an eye exam."

Rhiann's cheeks heated and she looked away from the other woman. She wasn't blind. Of course she saw Patrick's appeal. Quite well, actually. Her priorities were just elsewhere at the moment.

"I *knew* you couldn't be oblivious to his charms."

Rhiann shook her head slightly. "My son deserves my undivided attention."

The nurse rolled her eyes. "He's sleeping. I promise you he will not notice if you're counting the tiles in that little room or stealing a kiss from his doctor. One's just a lot more fun."

A laugh escaped Rhiann, despite her intention to show less emotion.

"I need to get back to my son," she said.

It was both an excuse to escape the awkward conversation and the honest truth. She was itching to get back to Levi. To make sure the monitors all had the same readouts and his little heart was still beating. But she also really wanted this impromptu chat to be over.

"Really, I do."

"Okay, but think about what I said." The nurse gave Rhiann's arm a gentle squeeze. "For what it's worth, I'm glad to see someone crack through that ice around his heart."

Rhiann smiled and murmured something in reply, but she wasn't even sure what. She hurried up the hall to her son's room and made a bit more noise than she had earlier. She wanted Patrick to have the opportunity to tell her his feelings on his own terms—not because she'd forced his hand.

When she walked into Levi's room Patrick smiled at her a little sheepishly. She took pity on him and pretended she hadn't heard a word.

"How's Levi?" She moved over to the crib and touched her baby's soft skin. "I just had to get a shower and some clean clothes. I was smelling pretty rank."

He wrapped his arms around her, nuzzling her

cheek with his nose. "Mmm… Not a problem anymore. You smell amazing to me."

"Patrick…"

"Levi's okay. I think he should be able to come off the vent by tomorrow morning. I've put in orders for them to wean him off it. So long as there aren't any hang-ups along the way, the goal is tomorrow morning."

His breath was warm in her ear and the heat from his hand splayed on her stomach was delicious.

A tap on the door behind them sent Patrick jerking away from her. Another of the nurses stood there, her face as pink as the cartoon characters on her scrub top.

"Um… Sorry… Dr. Scott, could you take a look at Dr. Whitehurst's patient in 5116? I've got a call out to Dr. Whitehurst but he hasn't called me back yet. One of the other nurses said you were in here, but I…uh… I didn't mean to interrupt."

She spoke to the floor about three feet in front of Patrick's shoes.

"It's fine, Carrie. I'll be there in one second."

She nodded and left in a hurry, without making eye contact.

Rhiann laughed. "Well, look who just got caught making out beneath the bleachers."

Patrick pulled her to him briefly. His lips barely touched her forehead.

"I'd better go check on this kid. Then I'll be back, and we'll see how Levi does after turning that vent down."

CHAPTER SIXTEEN

Rhiann

SEEING LEVI WITHOUT the vent had sent a wave of relief over Rhiann. Finally, she let herself relax a little—let herself think that everything might be okay. She brushed his hair away from his face, tears in her eyes as she watched him.

"The sedation should wear off soon. We've had to keep him sedated because of the vent, but now that he's off it we can let him wake up. He may be pretty fussy, because his chest's going to hurt. But that's to be expected."

"Thanks, Patrick," she said, without looking up.

"He isn't out of the woods yet, but his numbers are looking good so far."

He stepped up close to her and she could feel his body heat along the length of her spine.

"You're looking pretty good too…"

She elbowed him in the stomach lightly. "Nice

try, Doc, but your sweet-talking isn't going to work on me today. I could pass for an extra in a zombie movie, and we both know it."

"Looking tired doesn't make you any less beautiful."

"Hush!"

She sighed. Patrick was saying all the right things, even doing all the right things. He'd been attentive to both her and Levi. He'd worried about her well-being and made sure she ate, even when she hadn't wanted to think about food. But the timing just wasn't right.

"I need to focus on Levi right now. Can you just hold those thoughts until he's doing better?"

He wrapped his arms around her and rested his head on hers. "I suppose…"

She gave a small sigh.

"Were you alone when Levi was born?" Patrick asked, his entreaty soft and tentative.

She blinked away tears. "I wasn't alone the entire time. Charlie showed up to check on me, and when he realized I was all alone he refused to leave. He ended up holding my hand and seeing far more of me than a partner should, but he stayed by my side. He's the closest thing to a grandparent that Levi has."

Patrick's voice sounded taut when he replied, "I'm glad he was there for you."

"Me too." She turned to face him. "But it

made me stronger. It taught me that I didn't really need anyone else. When you don't rely on anyone, no one can let you down or hurt you."

He winced. "That's a pretty hard-hearted take on life."

"That's reality." She shrugged. "Everyone lets you down sooner or later. It doesn't shock or surprise me anymore because it's happened so often. Now it just makes me mad if I let myself get into that position in the first place."

"Rhiann—"

"You know, it's the people who make promises of forever that hurt the most. Pete promised me for better or worse, in sickness and in health, and he took off as soon as we found out Levi was sick."

Pete had hurt her, for sure, but the hurt of her broken marriage was something she could get past. Marriages sometimes ended. Relationships sometimes didn't work out.

Losing her best friend of so many years had caused far more damage to her ability to trust.

She tilted her head and bit her lip for a moment, wondering if she should voice that truth before saying, "And you... I'd say it was ironic, how fast you cut me out of your life for things that were out of my control, but there was no irony in it. Only shattered trust and the affirmation that I shouldn't expect even friendship to last forever."

He took her hand and she could see the struggle on his face as he tried to find words.

"Rhiann, I was broken. Losing Mallory…" he paused to swallow "…and Everly totally broke me. I lashed out at you because you were the one person I *could* blame. I was so…just so angry with life. Angry with myself for not being there for them, with you for not saving them, with Mallory for leaving me. I could barely function. Taking it out on you was not how I should have handled it, I know. But at the time I couldn't see that. Until very recently I couldn't see that."

She pulled her hand away to swipe at a tear running down her cheek. "The past is the past, right?"

"I owe you an apology for all that transpired. I know I can't ever make amends for the hurt that I've caused you."

She waved a hand in the direction of the crib, where her son was starting to stir. "Fixing his heart is enough for me. I don't know what it's like to lose a child, and I hope I never have to find out. I know what it's like to watch your child grow sicker and sicker, though. And this is the healthiest that Levi has looked in months. I would forgive anyone anything if it would make him better."

Patrick

His heart pounded in his chest as her words washed over him. She'd forgive anyone anything if it made Levi better.

Including him?

Taking a step back, Patrick inhaled a deep breath. Rhiann hadn't truly forgiven him, and maybe he didn't deserve her forgiveness.

Swallowing hard, he wished he could punch away the little voice screaming in his head that he *needed* her forgiveness. This was exactly why he didn't want anyone else getting close to him. People got close and then they had the ability to hurt him.

He blinked back what felt suspiciously like tears and strode from the room before he let it slip that her every word was slicing at his heart with a dull scalpel, leaving the type of ragged edges surgeons hated to stitch.

His hand shook as he punched the elevator button. When the elevator took too long he headed for the stairs, jogging down them and wishing that the physical exertion would help him expel the nerves and agitation saturating his body.

When his phone buzzed in his pocket he pulled it out to check the message—from Levi's nurse, who was worried about him. He took the stairs back up two at a time and was nearly out of breath when he made it to the pediatric cardiology floor.

Levi's room was filled with nurses. The charge nurse met his eyes and shook her head. "Dr. Scott, I don't think he was ready to come off the vent."

He squeezed the bridge of his nose. "Let's intubate him again."

Rhiann stepped up to him, hands fisted at her sides. "Can't you give him some more time? Maybe he just has to get used to not having help?"

He reached for her hand, and when she pulled away his soul felt her rejection. "His O2 levels are dropping and his heart-rate is fluctuating because he's having trouble breathing. He needs to be intubated to take some of the strain off his heart."

Moving to the sink, he washed his hands. As he was drying them, Rhiann spun him to face her. Her eyes were filled with tears and she snapped at him.

"Are you doing this because of what I said earlier? That's petty—even for you."

Shoulders back, posture rigid, Patrick towered over her and narrowed his eyes as he spoke.

"If you think that's the kind of man I am we have nothing left to say to each other beyond discussing Levi's care. You may be his mother, but I am his doctor. And I say he needs to be intubated. That has absolutely nothing to do with you and is one hundred percent because he needs it. Now, back away so that we can take care of Levi or I will have you escorted from this building."

She backed into the corner, her hand over her mouth, and he turned his attention from her to the little one struggling to breathe in front of him.

"Give me an ET tube."

CHAPTER SEVENTEEN

Patrick

FORTY-EIGHT HOURS passed before he was willing to take Levi off the vent again.

Time was a funny thing. That same forty-eight-hour stretch would pass all too quickly for someone enjoying a few days off work, but it would be excruciatingly long to a parent watching over a sick child.

Patrick found himself thinking it might have been the longest two days in his life. Longer even than when he'd lost his wife and daughter.

But it had to be even worse for Rhiann, he thought as he headed in after another night with little sleep.

He'd left the hospital at the end of visiting hours and now he was back early for rounds. He could probably push and stay later, but he had to work with those nurses regularly and he didn't want to get on their bad sides.

He didn't want to think about what they might be saying about him after he'd got caught with Rhiann in his arms and then got into a fight with her in a room full of nurses only a few hours later.

Rhiann was barely speaking to him. Every word was rationed, and their conversations were stilted, perfunctory, and only about Levi.

He stepped into the elevator and punched the number five. The doors had almost closed when he heard Clay call out, "Hold the elevator!"

Reaching out, he jabbed at the "open doors" button. The doors shuddered before opening wide once more.

"Thanks, man," Clay said with a bit of a huff as he joined Patrick in the elevator car. "I'm dragging this morning. Got rounds before a long day of appointments."

"I was going to check in on your Tricuspid Atresia kid this morning."

Clay leaned into the corner and sighed. "I'm worried about that one. The repairs look good. On the ultrasound everything looks like it should. But he's just not recovering like I'd hoped."

"I hear that." Patrick exhaled loudly, his cheeks puffing with the effort. "I'm going to try to extubate Levi again this morning. But I gotta tell ya I'm worried."

The elevator dinged and the doors opened on the fifth floor.

"Grab some coffee with me and we'll go round together. You look like you could use a friend this morning." Clay jerked his head toward the break room. "My treat."

Patrick shook his head impatiently. "Coffee's free here, moron."

"Why do you think I offered to pay for it?" Clay smirked. "Come on. Please?"

With a shrug, Patrick fell into step with Clay and they moved down the hall together. "How late were you out last night?" he asked his partner.

Clay opened the door to the staff lounge. He stopped halfway in the door to look at Patrick. "You always assume I was out. I'll have you know last night I was in by ten p.m."

"Date didn't go well?"

He shrugged. "Reached a point in the relationship where I needed more than a flexible pair of legs and she just didn't have anything to offer."

Patrick couldn't really relate to Clay's constant dating, the endless search for the perfect woman. He'd found two women in his life he'd been able to see himself having a future with and had been tempted very little beyond that.

Clay poured two coffees and held one out to

Patrick. When he saw his partner's eyes light up with amusement, Patrick's back went up in preparation.

"You wanna hear the rumors circulating around this place?"

Busying himself with adding cream and sugar to his coffee, Patrick replied, "Probably not, but I'm sure you're going to tell me anyways."

Clay grinned. "I hear tell of how a pretty little paramedic and her tiny son have melted the Ice Castle into a slushy puddle of goo."

Patrick shook his head. "You should know better than to listen to gossip."

"Oh, I have it on good authority that you've not only been caught kissing a patient's mama at said patient's bedside, but that you've made promises to that sweet baby that have had ovaries bursting all over this floor. There's gonna be a mess of babies born in nine months that *you* are directly responsible for." He clapped Patrick on the shoulder with a laugh.

Sinking down onto one of the couches, Patrick hung his head a bit. Someone had heard his bedside confessional? *Damn.* Now it would be spreading around the hospital like a wildfire. Hopefully the rumors wouldn't reach Rhiann before he got her speaking to him again.

Clay kicked at his shoe and Patrick grunted before looking up at him.

"Dude, you and Rhiann have always been the end game. I know you loved Mallory, but Rhiann's your soul mate."

"I know."

"So the rumors *are* true!" Clay's smile was so wide you could drive a semi through it. "Good."

Patrick ignored his partner and stared down into his cup full of coffee. He'd never thought of it in terms of Rhiann being his soul mate. He'd had a massive crush on her for years, of course. From the day they'd met up until the day he met Mallory, to be exact. Surprisingly, the terminology didn't feel wrong, though.

"You know they've stopped calling you Ice Castle, right?"

"Never asked them to call me that to start with," Patrick replied gruffly.

Clay stole a brownie out of a box on the table. "Now they're calling you Fudge Brownie, because you're all gooey where it counts."

Patrick leaned back and rubbed his eyes. Sometimes he hated this place, and the gossip culture that seemed forged into its very structure. Every hospital was the same, though. The staff thrived on whatever juicy tidbit they could pass along, whatever rumor they could spread at the change of shift.

He hated being the center of that kind of chatter.

Fudge Brownie. He'd never live the indignity of that one down. At least Ice Castle had earned him some respect.

Tossing the now lukewarm coffee, he followed Clay out the door. "What do you think they'll call me if she never speaks to me again?"

Rhiann

Once Levi had been extubated for the second time, and for two solid days had shown not only no regression but strong improvement, Rhiann let herself relax the slightest bit while Levi slept. The worried vibe in her gut had finally begun to ease.

She stared out the narrow window, with its soulless view of the hospital roof and the side of the adult hospital next door. If she pressed her face to the frigid glass, the corner of the parking garage came into view.

At least this room had some natural light. Often they hadn't been that lucky.

While she gazed down at the layer of tiny brown pebbles covering the roof, she let her thoughts drift away to a future she wanted but dared not speak of. A future where Patrick played a big role in her life as well as Levi's.

The only upside to this hellish week was that Patrick had been close by, to break up the monotony of the days. Well, besides the obvious fact that Levi was still alive.

Of course spending so much time with Patrick also had a downside…

Namely, she had dug herself into a hole she'd never get out of by falling in love with him. It didn't matter that their friendship had been on the rocks for a while. It didn't matter that she should be focused solely on Levi. When Patrick was around she found herself distracted by the gorgeous cardiac surgeon with the heart-stopping grin.

She had no defense against the way her heart reacted to the sight of him holding her son. And now it looked like she'd ruined that by speaking before she thought.

"Knock-knock," a soft voice called from the open door behind her.

She spun around to see Marilyn Scott in the doorway, with a small toy bear in her hands.

"I saw this little guy and couldn't help but get him for Levi."

"Thanks, but you really don't have to keep bringing him things."

It was the fourth little gift she'd brought for Levi this week. He had a stuffed dragon made of red and orange corduroy, a wooden firetruck, and a colorful new storybook as her earlier offerings.

Marilyn sat the bear in the crib next to Levi and ran a hand over his hair. "Of course I do. I'm behind on spoiling him."

Since Levi's surgery Patrick's mother had made her intention of stepping in as Levi's grandmother crystal-clear. She doted on him when he was awake, celebrating his every tiny accomplishment nearly as much as Rhiann herself. And when the baby was asleep Marilyn prayed over him with a fervor that made Rhiann wistful.

She'd lost her own mother several years back, and with Pete's parents out of the picture too Levi had never known the love of a grandmother. The closest thing he had to extended family was Charlie, who was more about tickles and fart noises than prayers and gentle caresses.

And, of course, Marilyn had made her opinion on Rhiann and Patrick tiptoeing around each other just as clear. She was enthusiastically cheering them on, her hints as unsubtle as permanent marker on white paper.

Rhiann's instinct was to deny any feelings on either side, her pulse racing each time. But her heart tended to skip beats, and every inch of her was very aware when Patrick was near. Her heated blushes most likely gave her away, but she still maintained they were merely friends.

Although these last few days, she wasn't even sure she could truthfully call them that.

"How's our little man doing today?" Marilyn asked.

"Patrick said he might get to go home tomorrow, actually," Rhiann told her with a genuine smile. "He's doing great. He's still sleeping a lot, but he stood up this morning, and even took a few steps around the edge of the crib. He's getting upset about the IV, though, so we've had to start watching him like a hawk when he's awake to keep him from pulling it out."

Marilyn snorted. "The boy has to make up for all the mischief he's missed out on while he's been sick. He'll be climbing walls before you know it."

Rhiann closed her eyes briefly on a prayer. "I'll never complain about his activity level—and that's a promise."

"Ah, but I bet you might have a word or two to say about the mischief he'll make. Lord only knows how much Patrick got into as a child. I wish some days for a little of that mischief to return. Now he's grown up on me. Sometimes I think I should have had a dozen kids, so that I wouldn't have so much free time now." She sighed—a long, sad sound. "But wishes aren't worth the paper they're written on, are they?"

Rhiann smiled sadly in commiseration. She'd

always wanted to have several children, but she wasn't sure that would happen now, given her current relationship status. "I don't know if Levi will ever have a sibling, but maybe someday."

Marilyn winked at her. "I have faith."

She hugged the older woman. "Thank you. For your faith and for being here this week."

"Where else would I be?"

A tap on the doorframe brought Rhiann's head around.

"Charlie!" She moved away from Marilyn to pull her partner in for a hug. "I wondered when you'd get around to showing your ugly mug."

"Some of us have jobs," he teased, tugging at a lock of Rhiann's hair. "You know, I don't think I've ever seen you with your hair down…"

"It's good to see you again, Charlie." Marilyn nodded at him.

Charlie smiled a mega-watt smile at the older woman. "Trust me, Mrs. Scott, it's my pleasure."

Patrick's mom returned his smile with one of her own. "I've been meaning to ask…how did the fundraiser turn out? There was quite a crowd, so I imagine it went well."

Charlie nodded, and Rhiann felt her eyes welling up in memory of the community's kindness.

"Better than I even expected. It was enough to pay off Levi's old medical bills and make a start on the new ones."

"That's wonderful news!" Marilyn clapped her hands in exclamation and then sent a worried look over to the crib, to make sure she hadn't woken Levi. When the baby didn't flinch she continued, her voice softer, "I'm so glad to hear it."

"I couldn't believe the turnout." Rhiann sighed, still overwhelmed at the amount of people who'd come out to show their support.

"I can," Charlie said, as he propped a shoulder against the narrow window, blocking most of the natural light. "You do so much for others that you shouldn't really be surprised when they return the favor in your hour of need."

Rhiann shook her head, feeling heat rising into her face as she blushed at Charlie's praise. "I only do my job…"

Charlie snorted. "That job means the world to a lot of people, and they were more than happy to show you just how much."

"Do you know how much I cried that night?" Rhiann tucked a long strand of hair behind her ear. "Each and every person who came up to me made me cry, I think."

"You should be proud of the impact you've had in their lives. I know I'm certainly proud of you and all that you've accomplished." Marilyn hugged her close. "Now, I have a meeting to get to, but I'll see you tomorrow. Kiss Levi for me when he wakes."

Marilyn waved as she left.

Rhiann turned to Charlie. "What brings you by today?"

"Can't a man come see his favorite girl without his motives being suspect?"

Rhiann was shaking her head at him, smiling widely, when movement in the doorway caught her eye.

CHAPTER EIGHTEEN

Patrick

HE'D GOTTEN INTO the habit of ending his rounds with Levi. Most days Rhiann was alone. A couple times his mom had been there. Once the babysitter had been visiting, but she'd left quickly after stuttering out a mumbled apology.

Finding another man in the room was *not* something he had expected. And seeing her smile at that man stabbed him right in the gut and twisted him up in knots a sailor would have been proud of.

He swallowed down the ball of envy lodged in his throat and tried to plaster a smile on his face when Rhiann looked up and they made eye contact. He wanted her to look at *him* with a smile on her face. He wanted to see those little dimples that only came out when she laughed showing up at *his* dark and sarcastic humor.

"Patrick!"

He moved quickly to Levi's side. "How's he been today?"

She followed him over to the crib and watched as he listened to Levi's heart and lungs.

Patrick closed his eyes and shut out Rhiann and the emotions of the moment. Once he'd calmed himself, he listened to the satisfying sounds coming from the baby's chest. Finally he was willing to call the surgery a success, because everything sounded perfect. Levi's coloring looked good, and he'd lost the blue tint to his lips and hands.

"He's been good. Still sleeping a lot, but he's eaten better than he *ever* has at all his meals today. He even toddled around the edge of the crib some."

With a gentle touch, he ran his hand over Levi's hair. His arms ached to pick the little one up and let him snuggle into his chest again.

"Good. As long as he doesn't have a setback tonight, I think we can get him out of here in the morning."

Even as he said it, he wanted to take it back. As long as Levi was in the hospital he had easy access to him—and to Rhiann. Once she took Levi home, though, he wouldn't have any reason to see them every day. But he couldn't hold Levi's progress back for personal reasons.

"That's great news!" the other man in the room said, drawing Patrick and Rhiann's attention back to him. "I know you're ready to get home."

Patrick's grip tightened around his stethoscope. He didn't like the familiarity in the other man's tone. Or how comfortable he looked in Rhiann's presence. He didn't like it because he felt excluded. Rhiann clearly considered Charlie family now, and he'd once been counted in that rank. Until a few days ago he had thought he might be again…

Rhiann smiled at Charlie like he'd just said the most brilliant thing in the world. "I still won't be back to work for a while, though, if I can swing the finances."

"Right. But a man can hope. I'd just about kill to get a steady partner again. I'm getting too old for this new-partner-each-day nonsense, you know."

"I'll be back when I'm back, Charlie," she said with a smirk.

And Patrick saw her eyes light with mischief. The type of mischief that she'd used to aim at *him*.

"Besides, getting me back isn't going to change the fact that you're getting old," she teased.

"Ain't that the truth?" The older man snorted.

"Well, I'm going to take my old self home for the night. Four a.m. will be here all too soon."

"Thank you for coming by," Rhiann told him softly. Then she stepped into his arms and allowed him to pull her close for a goodbye hug.

Patrick tried not to watch. He didn't need to torture himself with seeing Rhiann in the other man's arms. But he couldn't tear his eyes away. There was nothing sexual about it—nothing that even hinted at anything beyond a close friendship—but it still hurt that he'd lost that closeness with her.

Charlie stepped over and stuck his hand out to shake Patrick's. "I want to thank you for taking care of Rhiann and her little man. It means a lot to me."

Patrick shook his hand. "They mean a lot to me too."

Charlie smiled widely at him, understanding the meaning behind Patrick's declaration. He nodded at him. "Good. Y'all have a good night."

With Charlie gone, the silence stretched between him and Rhiann, hanging awkwardly while he tried to find words that might ease the awkwardness.

"Do you really think he can go home tomorrow?" she asked.

"That's my hope." He tapped his fingers

against his thigh. "And pretty soon you won't have to see me again. You won't have to pretend to forgive me, or act as though you like me, when inside you're cringing at my touch."

She stared at him, an incredulous look on her face. "Is that what you think I want?"

"I have no idea what you really want. Every time I think things are on track between us suddenly—*bam!*—we're hemorrhaging emotions and I can't find the bleeder." He ran a hand through his hair. "I know what *I* want, but I'm not sure it's compatible with this new-found desperation of yours to be on your own."

He swallowed hard.

"Somehow you and Levi broke through my defenses, and despite my vow never to let anyone close enough to hurt me again, here I stand, my heart racing like a teenage boy's, telling the girl he's crushing on that he likes her and praying she doesn't laugh in his face."

Arms wrapped around herself, she said, "Do I look like I'm laughing? Does the idea of being with me sound like a joke to you?"

The tiniest tendril of hope wrapped around his heart.

He stepped forward and laid a hand on her shoulder, but she pulled away.

Rhiann

Going to stand by the window, Rhiann stared out over the small section of roof, wishing there was a better view. Wishing there was somewhere she could go in this tiny room that would allow her to put a little distance between them at that moment.

When Patrick touched her she had problems thinking clearly. And she needed to think clearly if they were to move forward with any sort of relationship.

"Rhiann, no." He moved up behind her, his hands skimming up her arms from wrist to bicep. "Look at it from my perspective. I thought we were moving forward. We were getting along again. The chemistry between us could start fires. And yet… And yet there's a gap between us that you won't let me breach."

"I don't want to get hurt again."

Patrick kissed the side of her throat. "I know that."

His lips hovered over her pulse and she arched her neck to allow him better access.

"Please," she begged him, not even certain herself if she was asking him for more or to stop.

When his mouth suckled gently at the pulse-point in her throat all her thoughts were scrambled into a nonsensical mess. His touch turned her from a level-headed paramedic, a strong single mother, into a fangirl who had just met her favorite celebrity.

But all too soon he pulled away.

"This isn't the place or the time," he said, by way of apology for ending something that had such exquisite potential.

He was right, of course. And they had a lot to talk about before they took things further.

But before she could bring that up Levi started to stir.

"Levi's waking up," she said, pushing away from the window and moving to her son's side, switching her focus from Patrick to Levi. "Hello, sleepyhead, did you have a good nap?"

She brushed his shaggy hair out of his eyes. Once he was feeling a little better she'd have to take him in for his first haircut—a milestone she hadn't been sure he'd reach. But every day his color improved, and all hint of blue was gone from his lips and fingertips now. Levi was growing stronger by the minute, and the new potential for him filled her with such hope.

He raised his little arms to her, wanting a cuddle.

She lowered the rail on the crib and picked him up carefully, so as not to irritate his incision. He snuggled into her chest and went to pop a thumb into his mouth, frowning when his eyes landed on the IV in his hand. He reached for it with his other hand.

"Not quite yet, little guy," Patrick said, with a hint of amusement in his voice as he blocked Levi's access to the IV. "I'll get a nurse to go ahead and take that out for you, though, since it's bothering you so much.

"You can't do it?" Rhiann asked.

He tickled Levi's side gently. "I don't want him to connect me with anything painful, so I'd rather not."

She raised an eyebrow at him. "You did his surgery."

"Yeah, and he was sound asleep, with no idea that I was the one holding the scalpel that sliced through his precious skin. He's awake now. Completely different situation."

"You big softie."

She squeezed Patrick's hand. His gentleness with Levi made her fall for him a little more each time she saw the two of them together. Each smile he bestowed upon her son found one more chink in the armor around her heart.

"Only when it comes to you two." He winked at her. "I'll be back."

She watched Patrick leave before turning her attention back to Levi. "You need to leave that IV alone, baby. You wanna play? Look at this bear!" She grabbed the little brown teddy that

Patrick's mom had brought by earlier. "Look at this guy. He's convinced someone that he needs to come live with you—can you believe that?"

She paused, and Levi babbled a bit.

"Of *course* you can believe that. Why *wouldn't* he want to come live with you? I know. Mommy's silly for even thinking that was unbelievable."

She made the bear dance in front of Levi. He kept his eyes on the bear with a smile on his face, and the occasional laugh snuck out. It kept him distracted from the IV for the moment too.

Rhiann couldn't have kept the smile off her face if she'd tried. Love for Levi filled her to overflowing, and his happiness made her so joyous it could hardly be contained.

When Patrick came back in with a nurse, Levi beamed a radiant smile at him. He reached out for Patrick to pick him up, and Patrick did so without hesitation.

"Someone woke up in a good mood," Patrick said, hugging Levi close.

Levi chattered at him in a string of unintelligible noises.

Patrick treated the conversation seriously. "Your bear is a crazy dancer, you say? Has your mommy been giving him lessons? She's one of the most enthusiastically bad dancers I know. I'll have to tell you a story about our senior prom. It involves a wardrobe malfunction, five stitches, and a set of lost car keys—but that's a story for another time."

The nurse snorted and then tried unsuccessfully to cover the sound. She kept her head down while she got the bandage and supplies ready to remove Levi's IV.

"All right, Mr. Levi, you ready to get that IV out?" the nurse asked him.

Levi loved it when the nurses came in and talked to him. He couldn't get enough attention—particularly from the younger nurses. He giggled and waved at her.

"I'm gonna take that as a yes." She turned to Patrick. "You wanna sit down here with him, so you can hold him still?"

Patrick sank down into the avocado-colored recliner and the nurse made quick work of taking the IV out. In less than a minute it was gone, and Levi had a brightly colored *Sesame Street* bandage in its place. The few tears he'd thought about crying had soon dried up when he'd been handed a pink popsicle.

The nurse cleaned up and then removed her gloves with a snap. "I'll be in later to check on him."

Levi relaxed against Patrick, happily slurping on the popsicle in his hand, the very picture of contentment. And Rhiann had to admit Patrick looked quite content too.

"He looks happy there with you."

Patrick grinned up at her, his eyes bright. "I'm pretty happy here with him too."

While she meant every syllable of what she'd said, the next phrase that came out of her mouth surprised them both.

"I love you."

CHAPTER NINETEEN

Rhiann

THE NIGHT PASSED fitfully for Rhiann. Levi slept through without a peep, but she tossed and turned on the lumpy reclining chair without much rest. Her mind would not shut off long enough to let her sleep. Patrick's sudden departure the night before had her worrying she'd pushed too far, too fast, even though her rational mind knew that he'd been called to see another patient.

She'd already lost too many people in her life. With her own mom long gone, and no dad to speak of, Levi, Patrick and Charlie were all she had.

Besides Levi, Patrick was the most important person in her life. She couldn't bear to lose him again.

Clearly Patrick had not expected her to blurt

out an admission of love. She hadn't exactly expected it herself.

Oh, she'd always loved him as her best friend. But now she loved him with the heart of a woman who had known loss. Loved him as the man she wanted to spend her life with.

When residents and doctors started coming down the hall Rhiann finally gave up on trying to sleep and got dressed for the day. Patrick had said Levi could go home this morning, and she was more than ready to get out of the hospital. Maybe in her own bed tonight she'd actually sleep.

She packed all Levi's things while she waited for him to wake up, tucking all the stuffed animals that Patrick's mom had brought him into the diaper bag.

When Levi woke, Rhiann changed his diaper and put a fresh shirt on him.

"Mommy will get you a proper bath once we get home," she promised him. "Between me and you, I don't really want to take you back to that dingy old apartment—but it's home, I guess. Sometime soon Mommy will get you a better place to live. Somehow…"

She looked up to find Patrick leaning against the doorframe. Heat flooded her face as she wondered how much of her little confession he'd heard, but she held her head high. Not having the funds for a nicer place was something out of her control at the moment, but maybe with Levi finally healthy she could start saving toward a better apartment.

"You ready to bust out of this prison?"

"Beyond ready."

He rolled his eyes and strode forward. "I was talking to Levi."

"I think I can speak for him on this matter."

Patrick handed her some papers. "His release paperwork. The nurse will be in in a moment to go over it with you—hospital rules."

Rhiann flipped through the sheets. Diet, exercise, wound care... Standard stuff. Nothing concerning. She laid the paperwork on top of Levi's bag.

Patrick stood next to the crib, tickling Levi and making faces at him. Levi laughed and didn't even have a coughing fit. He was truly on his way to being healthy, thanks to Patrick, which was giving her one more reason to fall for the man.

If Patrick Scott looked over at her and they made eye contact there was no way he wouldn't see the love that must surely be shining from her eyes like a lighthouse, beckoning him to her, and that might send him running again. So she busied herself double-checking that she'd packed all Levi's things.

With focused determination she scanned every inch of the hospital room, looking for any item that might have escaped her initial perusal.

"You okay?" Patrick asked, wrapping his arms around her from behind.

"Mmm-hmm." She tried not to melt into his arms—really, she did. But her body had other plans and she found herself leaning into the delicious warmth of his touch. "Just ready to take Levi home."

"You wouldn't be trying to get away from me, would you?"

She shook her head, unable to put her voice to words for fear that her true feelings would come tumbling out with no stopping them.

"Good. I have a surprise for you when we leave here."

Curiosity got the best of her and she looked up at him and made eye contact, despite her concerns.

"I'm not telling you what. You'll just have to wait."

He flashed her a grin that made her heart do crazy things. But the nurse came in to go over the discharge instructions before Rhiann could question Patrick about what he had planned.

Within a few minutes Levi was officially discharged, and he was tucked safely into the back of Patrick's car only a short while after that.

"I don't know why you wouldn't let me drive myself home. You'll have to take me back to the hospital to get my car at some point."

Patrick hadn't got on the interstate to head toward her apartment, she noticed. Instead, he drove out past Vanderbilt and toward Green Hills. She watched the houses and businesses go by.

"Where are you taking us?" she asked finally.

"You'll see." Patrick reached over and took her hand in his. "You trust me, right?"

"Yes…" she said, dragging the single syllable out to the length of three.

But she sank back into the seat and tried to ignore the sweet sensation of his thumb grazing over the palm of her hand.

Lush vegetation nearly hid the driveway Patrick turned in to. Rhiann sat up straighter and examined their surroundings. The narrow lane opened to a small yard and then the most adorable little cottage, with trim that looked like gingerbread.

"Where are we?"

"Home."

"You moved?"

He nodded. "That modern half-glass monstrosity downtown was all Mallory. I never did like it. And with her and Everly gone all those reflective surfaces did was show me how alone I was. This is as far I as I could get from that."

Traditional architecture had always held sway over Rhiann. She'd take a stately old Victorian over a high-rise condo any day. Or, in this case, a cozy cottage over crazy modern angles. With the addition of a few chairs or rockers she could picture spending a lot of time sitting on that porch, watching Levi play. And with just a little work the already secluded yard could be transformed into the perfect oasis away from the stresses of working in the medical field.

"I love it."

Grinning at her, he opened the car door. "I was hoping you'd say that. Now, let's get our boy inside."

Our boy.

Like before, hearing Patrick claim Levi sent Rhiann's heart into a frenzy.

If only…

Patrick

With Levi in his arms, Patrick led Rhiann up the steps and into the little cottage he'd bought after losing Mallory and Everly. His realtor had hit a game-winning home run with this place. He'd told the guy he wanted something the complete opposite of the modern house he'd lived in with his late wife and this had been the first house he'd been shown.

He loved the character of the little house. It had a welcoming charm that was missing from the sleek lines and crisp angles of modern architecture. The crown moldings and wide windows added a homey touch that had whispered *This is home* from his first step inside the front door.

Over the last three years he'd spent hours upon hours on the porch, just soaking up the healing silence he found here. The small acreage had proved to be the perfect buffer to drown out the hustle and bustle of the city around him.

Until today, his parents and Clay had been the only people he'd allowed to invade the sanctuary he'd created here. But with Rhiann, it didn't feel like she was invading—more like she was enhancing his space.

He watched her face, hoping she'd love the coziness as much as he did.

"This place…" she said. "Wow. Somehow you've found a house that's the architectural version of you."

He snorted. "What does *that* mean?"

She shrugged. "The view is nice from the outside, but the look maybe doesn't appeal to everyone. This house looks like it has frosting on the eaves, and you have frost in your eyes, but once you get past the frosty exterior you find a warm and welcoming heart that feels just a bit lonely. Strong bones, but empty without a family."

Patrick's breath caught. Every word she'd said fit like a glove, but he was hoping to change that last bit…

"Look again." He managed to get out the words, surprised when his voice didn't crack under the pressure.

"Hmm…?" She looked around, her eyes scanning for something she might have missed.

"Go down the hall a bit. Maybe try the first door on the left."

Confusion filled her eyes, but she did as he suggested. Patrick followed her with Levi in his arms. She opened the door cautiously—and then gasped as she peeked inside.

"Patrick!" She looked back at him, fat tears welling up in her eyes.

"Levi? You wanna play in your room while I talk to your mommy?"

His heart raced as he set Levi gently on the colorful rug just inside the door. He'd barely slept this week, trying to make the perfect bedroom for the little boy, filling it with cars and trucks and all the things a boy needed.

"You set up a room for Levi here?"

Her voice shook. The emotion in her eyes gave him hope that by the end of the day his house and his heart would no longer be missing a family.

"Of course I did. I want him to spend a lot of time here." He took one of her hands in his and tugged her into the room across the hall. "This is my office. We'll leave the door open so we can hear Levi, but there's a bit more privacy. I have a lot to say, and a nursery's not the ideal spot for it."

"Okay…"

"Sit."

He gently nudged her toward one of the wingback leather chairs. Once she'd sunk down onto the edge of the seat, he kneeled in front of her.

"Rhiann, I don't deserve your forgiveness, but I'm asking for it. I know that Mallory and Everly's deaths were not your fault. I know that—and maybe deep down I always did. But I blamed you for years because I needed a scapegoat. Because if I didn't blame you for their deaths then I'd have to look inward and take my share of the guilt. I've never admitted this to anyone before, but I was away at a conference the entire week before they died. I was supposed to come in the night before, but my flight got bumped. Rather than cancel or reschedule my appointments, I went straight to my office instead of going home to them."

"Patrick—"

"Let me finish." He took a deep breath. "When they called me to the ER, while Mallory was still in surgery, a doctor told me that if the paramedics had gotten her there sooner they'd have had a chance. I latched onto that phrase like it was the gospel. I used his words as reinforcement that *you* were to blame and not me. You, because you were there and couldn't save them—not me, because I should have been there. I thought that as a surgeon I would have seen the signs…"

She put her fingers over his mouth to stop him from talking. "You can't do that to yourself. No one was at fault. There was a bad wreck on the interstate that day. We had to go back and circle around through a neighborhood. It took us longer than was ideal to get to the hospital, yes, but the only way either of them could have been saved would have been if the obstetrician had caught the issues with the placenta before that day. Maybe—and this is a big maybe—maybe if it had happened at the hospital, where they could have been taken to the OR immediately, with the blood bank on standby… I tried—Patrick, you have to believe that I did everything I could that day—but I just couldn't save them. You couldn't have either."

He kissed her fingers before pulling them away from his mouth. "I know that now. And

I know that there was absolutely nothing you could have done to change the outcome for Mallory or Everly. I am so ashamed that I ever believed you hadn't done everything within your power to save them. You would have done everything for a stranger. Knowing they were my family and you couldn't save them had to have broken your heart. And then I pushed you away too."

"Of course I would have." She teared up. The raw pain in her eyes spoke of her sincerity. "I loved them too, you know. I was looking forward to being Auntie Rhiann to your daughter. I grieved their loss like I grieved for losing my best friend."

"Can you forgive me for the last three years?" He held his breath as he waited for her reply.

Rhiann

"There's nothing to forgive. I knew from the start you were just lashing out due to grief. I always hoped you'd come around—I was just trying to give you the space you needed to mourn."

She cupped his cheek with a shaking hand. Knowing she truly had her best friend back filled her heart with an overwhelming joy.

"There is a lot to be forgiven, actually, and I don't deserve a friend like you," said Patrick, and the storm in his blue eyes reflected the depth of his regret. His solemn expression added to the seriousness of his speech.

She teased him a bit, trying to lighten the somber mood. "I'm willing to put the past behind us so long as you promise never to be so stupid again."

"I'll try." He chuckled. "I'm gonna take a peek at Levi."

He walked to the doorway and looked across the hall. Rhiann wondered if he was seriously concerned with Levi's well-being at that moment or if he just needed a break from the serious conversation they were having.

Rhiann leaned back in the chair and watched him look in on Levi. "Is he okay?"

He looked over his shoulder and grinned. "He's sitting in the middle of the rug surrounded by alphabet blocks. We might have a future writer on our hands."

"You keep saying 'we' and 'our.'" She laughed, trying to not let her hopes grow too high. "You trying to lay claim to my son?"

"It's impossible not to love that little guy. I've fallen in love with him *and* with the idea of being his dad." He walked back over to her. "I'm pretty over the moon for his mommy too…"

"Patrick—"

He sank down on one knee in front of her.

"Rhiann Masters, I am head over heels in love with you. I know all too well how short life can be, and I don't want to wait another day to start our lives together."

His right hand fumbled in his pocket for a second before bringing out a small black box.

"Will you allow me the honor of being your husband and Levi's dad?"

"Yes." She leaned forward and sealed her answer with a kiss.

Their lips met and Rhiann would have sworn their souls entwined. When she'd walked into his office that day only a short time ago, scared but determined, she had only asked for Patrick to give her son a future. She'd had no idea how much bringing Patrick back into her life would change everything—and not just for Levi.

After Pete had raked her heart and soul over the scorching coals of heartbreak she'd sworn off men. Focused entirely on Levi, she'd dropped back from truly living into barely surviving without realizing.

Patrick's presence had opened her eyes to that.

Patrick had healed Levi's heart and somehow patched hers up along the way.

Patrick broke the kiss to slip a ring on her finger. "You haven't even looked at this ring. I could have put costume jewelry on your finger."

"I love you. What you put on my finger means

nothing compared to the love you've put in my heart."

"Sap," he teased, before brushing his lips across her forehead. "I love you. So, can I go play with my son now?"

"Go ahead."

Rhiann stood and watched as the man she loved gently picked up her son and tickled his sides. The love in his eyes matched the love in her heart.

She looked down at the beautiful ring on her finger and smiled.

Sometimes wishes did come true.

EPILOGUE

Three years later
Patrick

PATRICK SANK DOWN onto the grass and wiped a few blades of cut grass from the engraved marble.

"Hi, Mallory, Everly… I've brought someone for you guys to meet. Everly, this is your baby sister Arden. She's only a few days old, so I can't keep her out here long."

He shifted into a more comfortable position with Arden in his lap.

"I'll always miss you girls. And don't worry—I'll make sure to tell Arden all about you when she's old enough to understand."

"Daddy!"

He looked up to see Levi running full-force toward him. The four-year-old had made a complete recovery. Without seeing the scars on his chest, it was impossible to tell he'd ever had a heart problem.

"Hey, buddy."

Levi plopped down on the grass next to him. "I beat Mommy racing over here. But I think she let me win. She said we need to let you talk to the girls. But I think you don't want to be outnumbered." Levi gave him a little side-eyed grin. "Mommy doesn't know how boys think, does she?"

Patrick put an arm around his son and hugged him close, trying really hard not to laugh. "I'll always be happy to see you."

Levi reached over and tickled Arden. "Why doesn't she laugh yet?"

"She's too little."

He sighed. "She needs to hurry up and grow, because I need someone to play with."

Rhiann laughed as she walked up, catching only Levi's last statement. "I tried to keep him over by the car, but he's a little faster than I am at the moment. I didn't want him to disturb you. He was just antsy in the car."

"He's fine." He tousled Levi's blond hair. "Levi, do you think you can walk slowly back to the car with Mommy? Don't make her run, though, okay? Mommy needs to take it easy, like we talked about. I'll be right there."

When Rhiann held her hand out Levi took it

reluctantly. He looked over his shoulder at Patrick. "Okay, Daddy...but only 'cause you asked me."

Rhiann smiled softly at him before she walked Levi back to the car.

He put a hand on the headstone. "The first few years without you both I barely survived. I shut out the possibility of love. But then Rhiann and Levi came into my life and forced their way into my heart."

He looked across the carefully mown grass to where his beautiful wife was walking with his son. And then down to the baby sleeping in his lap.

"And now we have Arden."

The breeze picked up and carried to him a soft note of gardenia. He closed his eyes and inhaled deeply. The scent reminded him of the perfume Mallory used to wear, and he thought maybe it was a sign that she approved of how he'd moved on.

"I love you both. Goodbye."

When he reached the car, Rhiann asked, "Did you have a good chat?"

"Thank you."

"For what?" she asked, taking Arden from him for a quick cuddle before she buckled the baby into her car seat.

"For being you."

His arms surrounded her before she could move away from the open car door.

"For being my wife and understanding that my love for them doesn't mean I love you any less."

He leaned down.

Seconds before his lips touched hers he was interrupted.

"Are you guys gonna kiss *again*? Grandma says you-all kiss too much and that's where Arden came from. Can you go for a brother this time? Because I don't want another sister…"

"I'm game if you are," Patrick told her. "Or at least I'm up for a little practice."

"You wish!"

The contagious happy laugh that escaped from his wife was a joyous sound he wouldn't mind hearing every day of his life.

She laid her head on his shoulder and he kissed the top of her head.

"Every day."

* * * * *